I0573341

Deadly Family Secrets

A. C. Mason

A Wings ePress, Inc.
Mystery Novel

Wings ePress, Inc.

Edited by: Jeanne Smith
Copy Edited by: Heather O'Connor
Executive Editor: Jeanne Smith
Cover Artist: Trisha FitzGerald-Jung

Wings ePress Books
www.wingsepress.com

Published In the United States Of America

Wings ePress Inc.
3000 N. Rock Road
Newton, KS 67114

What They Are Saying About

Deadly Family Secrets

"Good to see Susan Foret back to solving crimes after the death of her husband in *Deadly Bayou*. Her empathy and knowledge of Louisiana life always bring about a satisfying ending for mystery lovers."

—Lynn Shurr, author of *The Longleigh Chronicles*

Dedication

In memory of our sweet Jennifer.
We lost you to cancer, but Heaven gained a beautiful new
angel.

* * *

For wisdom is better than rubies; and all things that may be desired cannot be compared to it.

—*Proverbs 8:11*

KJV

Haydel, Richard, LeBlanc Family Tree

Charles Haydel headed one of his father's businesses in British Burma for several years in the early to mid-1920s. He married **Harriet Blakewell** in Burma. A Burmese man sold Charles a fabulous ruby. According to Rangoon locals, the gem had been stolen from a religious shrine and therefore would curse anyone who had possession of the jewel. Charles believed the so-called curse was only native superstition. He died in 1930 as a result of a fall from the balcony of his home.

Harriet (Blakewell) Haydel was the daughter of British missionaries noted for their work with Burmese natives. Harriet gave birth to twin girls a short time before leaving with Charles and the girls to return to Louisiana.

Louise Haydel, Charles and Harriet's daughter; she died at age five in a horseback riding accident.

Ruth (Haydel) Richard, Louise's twin, married **Michael Richard;** she died of heart problems.

Anne (Richard) LeBlanc, daughter of Ruth and Michael, married **Carl LeBlanc;** she died in a hit-and-run auto accident.

Melanie LeBlanc, daughter of Anne and Carl, married and divorced **Brett Lassiter;** she went back to her maiden name after divorcing; was murdered. No one has ever been arrested in her death.

Tracy Lassiter, daughter of Melanie and Brett; she returns to Cypress Lake upon the reopening of her mother's cold case.

One

Allemand Parish, Louisiana
Monday, July 14

A hot breeze stirred the leaves of gnarled oak trees that surrounded the cemetery and dotted the entire property. In the distance, I spotted a dock on the bank of Petite Allemand Bayou, which flowed behind the land. I could see why Live Oak Landing made a fitting name for this place.

There had once been a large home on the property, described by locals as being the size of the White House in D.C. Over the years, the house had fallen into ruin and been torn down almost twenty years earlier. Descendants of the original owners from the Haydel, Richard, and LeBlanc families no longer resided in Allemand Parish, but it appeared someone saw fit to keep the grass cut and the cemetery weeded. A hired caretaker, perhaps.

I hesitated with my hand on the tall wrought iron gate. Should I go in? According to the posted signs plastered on the fence here and on the high stone wall around the adjacent acres, I would be trespassing.

I might get into trouble for entering this property, but for me, Susan Foret, nothing unusual. Besides, the lock on the main gate had been broken, most likely by other intruders, so I made up my mind and walked right in.

In many ways I've become like one of those female protagonists in mystery novels who is known as TSTL—too stupid to live. One who goes headlong into a known dangerous situation without thinking. But what could happen here?

By chance I had discovered a newspaper article about this family while researching my latest work-in-progress mystery novel. The last property owner, Melanie LeBlanc, had been murdered. After years of searching for her killer with no success, the detectives moved her homicide to the cold case files. The article also chronicled an eerie family history of deaths that some individuals believed related to a cursed ruby purchased in Burma sometime in the nineteen-twenties. Their story fascinated me and I wanted to know more.

The article displayed a photo of the house, which had been built in the late eighteen hundreds by a member of the Haydel family. I imagined how grand the home would have looked situated on all this land, and the many parties and dinners held by this high-society family.

The family cemetery—my reason for coming here—took up about a half-acre, tucked inside its own ornate iron fence. I paused to survey the graves that held departed members of the Haydel, Richard, and LeBlanc families.

Some of the older graves were simple, white, aboveground, coffin-like tombs. Behind those a large baroque-style tomb resembling a small house towered above the others. The name Haydel was etched in stone above the entrance.

The iron gate to the cemetery gave a loud creak as I opened it. I cringed and looked over my shoulder to check for anyone in the area who might have heard this sound. Of course, I didn't see anyone else around. I proceeded to check out the identities of those buried there.

The gravestones displayed names and dates for the people interred in the cemetery, but told nothing of their traumatic life stories. Most of the stones were tarnished by age and weather, including the most recent burial, that of Melanie LeBlanc. Below her name, a phrase written in flowery script identified her as the *Beloved Daughter of Carl and Anne Richard LeBlanc.*

A muffled crack, like someone stepping on a dry twig, startled me. The sound seemed to come from behind the Haydel tomb. Maybe I was wrong about no one else's being there.

A few minutes passed and I didn't detect any more sounds. Probably a squirrel searching for acorns. I shook off my feeling of dread and walked down the next row of graves, reading the names as I snapped a few pictures with my cell phone.

I continued walking and rounded the left side of the big tomb. Graffiti in bold black paint with red outlines spelled out the words *The Ruby* next to a pentagram, the five-pointed star usually associated with the occult. The paint looked wet, as if someone had painted the design only minutes ago. I took a photo of the "artwork," for lack of a better word.

How could anyone get a thrill by defacing property, especially on a gravestone? Cemeteries are sacred ground. Could there be more of this kind of trash on the rear of the tomb?

A thought occurred to me that sent my heart racing. *Please don't let there be a dead body waiting for me to discover.* On numerous occasions I'd been placed in a situation where someone was murdered near me, or I discovered the murder victim *in situ.* Chills moved up my spine. I cautiously peered around the corner and heaved a sigh of relief. No dead body.

A slight movement on the side of the tomb made me stop short. My breath caught in my throat. In a flash, a man jumped out, shooting a spray of black paint in my direction. I managed to make an evasive move in time for the paint to miss his intended target: my face.

The man sprinted toward the fence and leaped over it with the ease of a track star. Even with my heart beating a mile a minute, I still had the presence of mind to snap a photo of the retreating male figure.

He made his way toward a grove of trees near the dock and disappeared from view. A boat motor roared to life and soon faded into the distance. The track star appeared to have begun a graffiti vandalizing spree only minutes before I arrived on the scene. His choice of subjects for his artwork proved interesting, to say the least.

I decided to leave the premises before trouble visited me again or someone noticed my car parked outside the gate and came to investigate. And to add to anyone's suspicion of me, my blue capri pants and matching shirt were now sprinkled with black spots from the paint mist. This outfit seemed destined for the trash bin. I ran a hand through my hair to check for paint. Luckily, I didn't feel any. I'd check closer when I returned home.

In the past, my curiosity had gotten me into a lot of trouble, and this time intuition told me any further snooping probably would do so again. As I closed the main gate behind me, a marked vehicle belonging to the Allemand Parish Sheriff's Office pulled up next to mine. The driver side door opened and the so-far unidentified officer stepped out, his hand resting on the butt of his side-arm.

I squinted in the sun's glare, trying to decide if I should be worried about being arrested. Relief came over me when I recognized Ronnie Hart, the parish sheriff, who also happened to be one of my neighbors. I still had to explain why I had trespassed on private property and why my clothes revealed spots of black paint. At least he wasn't a deputy who didn't know me.

Ronnie eased his stance. "Susan, what are you doing here?"

I walked toward him, mulling over in my mind what I intended to say to explain my presence in a posted area. What the heck? The truth is always the best.

"Earlier today, while researching a subject for a mystery I'm working on, I discovered an old newspaper article about this place and its owners. My curiosity got the best of me, and I had to take a look at the cemetery."

"I take it you're aware of the no trespassing signs posted all over." He appeared to suppress a smile.

I looked him straight in the eye. "Yes, I did see them."

"Trespassing is against the law," he said in a stern voice. "I should write you a citation."

Could he really be serious? I asked him that very question.

He laughed. "No, you probably weren't up to anything that might be suspicious." His demeaner quickly changed. "I take that back. Do you have paint on your clothes?"

"Yes, it is paint. I didn't have any mischief in mind, but someone else did." I told him about my meeting with the graffiti artist and showed him the photos I'd snapped.

"You could've been hurt if that paint had made it into your eyes." Ronnie narrowed his gaze toward the gate. "Obviously he got on the property from the bayou. But how'd you get in the place? The main gate did have a chain with a padlock on it."

"Not anymore. I didn't see anything like a chain or any kind of lock. I simply opened the gate and walked right in."

"I'll get some of my deputies out here to check the property to make sure nothing else is amiss. Then I'll get in touch with the owner." He gave me the look my late husband Jim always threw at me when he thought I should leave well enough alone for my own good. "In the meantime, don't be snooping around out here. It's pretty isolated most of the time. This little episode should be a warning in itself. If something serious were to happen to you, it might be hours before anyone found you."

"Okay, I won't come back, but first, will you tell me the name of the current owner? It was my understanding the property is still owned by the descendants of Charles Haydel."

He thought a moment. "Yeah, Tracy Lassiter is the last remaining direct family member and is the sole owner of this property. She moved to Mobile after her mother's death. I'm pretty sure she can give you a lot of good information about the family history and about this supposedly cursed Burmese ruby." He came close to rolling his eyes.

"You don't believe in curses?" I asked with faux innocence. "There could be something to the story."

"No, the idea of a curse is only playing on the superstitions of others, but it makes a great plot for a horror novel."

Two

I couldn't possibly write a horror novel. The notion of demons, devils, evil spirits and other unworldly creatures possessing the body of a human being was terrifying to me. If I thought about it long enough, the murder and mayhem in today's society could be as scary as any horror novel or movie. But murderers were all real people, real human beings whose lives had taken a wrong turn. Although some may seem downright evil, they could all be dealt with in the justice system.

Ronnie might be correct in his opinion of curses. But I wondered if the idea of a hex could actually cause the "cursed" person to die. You know, the power of suggestion. I wanted to find out more about the Burmese ruby that had been passed down through at least four generations. Was Tracy Lassiter the current owner of the jewel? Or had she gotten rid of it in an attempt to stave off the curse?

I arrived home to an empty house, an oddity for me. Well, almost empty. Katy, my cat, announced herself with a soft meow and immediately rushed over to her food bowl. She seems to think that more food should be added if any part of the bowl is showing. I smiled and indulged her by adding a small amount of her favorite dry food.

My nine-year-old twins had left yesterday for three weeks of summer camp, this one especially for children of law enforcement personnel. The only reason Matthew and Caroline eagerly agreed to go was because their friends, Ronnie and Renee Hart's three children, were also attending.

I felt the need to tell someone about my adventure at the cemetery. Josh was the logical person I would tell these days. He wasn't here either. With him out of town for a training seminar, I didn't want to phone him unless I had an emergency, which I didn't. He had called last night to fill me in on his day's activities, but he wasn't scheduled to return until Friday. I missed seeing and talking to him.

Josh Broussard is a private investigator and a love interest. Although we aren't living together, we see each other a lot.

My true feelings for Josh are confusing, to say the least. The physical attraction is definitely there, but also a strong affection for him exists. I've tried to convince myself Jim would want me to move on with my life, but somehow, I can't take the step. Guess I need a sign from Jim in order to make the move.

I had recently agreed to help Josh in his office with paperwork and answering the phone. He wanted me to apply for a PI license so we could be partners in the business.

On the surface, that sounded like a great idea, but after I'd thought about it, I decided not to go for it. I'd have to learn how to use a gun. Guns scare me. This may seem strange for a woman who was married to a law enforcement officer for many years.

My reasons are simple. After last year's events involving Josh's shooting of a man right outside my bedroom door, and my kidnapping at gunpoint by members of the Gallagher family, I didn't particularly care for having a gun in the house.

Oh, and I could never forget the incident when Matthew and his best friend, Reed Hart, found the weapon used to kill Celina Baum in a swampy area where the killer had disposed of it.

The boys decided Matthew should hide the gun in his room because they wanted to have a gun like their fathers' to play cops and robbers.

I had been having a lot of trouble with Matthew around the one-year anniversary of the murder of my husband, Jim Foret, who at the time was the chief of police in the town of Cypress Lake. The second anniversary was coming up in a few weeks. I hated to think about the bad memories and the possibility of renewed trouble with Matthew. Perhaps since the kids wouldn't be in town for the anniversary, they might be spared the trauma. I could only hope.

I gave a mirthless chuckle. One good thing did happen today when I was nosing around in the cemetery: the only dead people in the area were officially buried. I didn't suddenly come across the body of a murder victim like I had so many times in the past.

Dismissing the last thought, I removed my paint-spotted clothing and went into the bathroom to shower. Standing under the warm spray, I went over in my mind the events at the cemetery.

I couldn't get the graffiti writer off my mind. He appeared to be in his late teens or early twenties. The pentagram is a usual graffiti subject for pranksters wanting to stir up panic in the area with rumors about devil worship or witchcraft. His approximate age would likely fit with drawing the pentagram.

The words *The Ruby* bothered me. Was the story of the curse common knowledge? Maybe I was jumping to conclusions.

After completing my shower and drying my hair, I went back to doing research on the Burmese ruby. An hour later, I still hadn't come across any new information about this particular jewel. Time to call on a local source. I didn't want to contact Tracy Lassiter yet. I had no logical or acceptable reason to do so at this time, except for my insatiable curiosity. I decided to walk next door to pick Rachel's brain about the families and the cursed jewel.

My neighbor greeted me at the door before I even knocked. "I happened to see you walking over here. What's up?"

"I'm interested in an event that happened back in two thousand one. Besides, it's lonely at my house and I need some company," I quickly added.

She raised an eyebrow. "If I didn't know you better, I would think I was being used for information."

My turn to laugh. "No way. You do know better."

"Come on in and have some coffee. I just made a fresh pot." She motioned with her hand for me to take a seat at the kitchen table.

Even though Rachel Marchand is old enough to be my mother, she remains my dearest friend. She and her husband Danny, the former Allemand Parish sheriff, had taken Jim and me under their wings when we first moved to Cypress Lake. I loved them both dearly.

"So, what event in that year has caught your interest?" She set two cups of steaming coffee on the table and sat across from me. "I'm sure it has to be a murder."

"You know me too well." I blew on the hot brew and took a sip. "The murder of Melanie LeBlanc."

She arched her brows. "How did you ever find out about her murder?"

I explained how I happened to come across an article about her death. "I'm fascinated not only by the case, but more so about the ruby and Melanie's family history regarding the idea the gem cursed its owners."

"Have you by some chance spoken to Remi today?"

"No, why do you ask?" She was referring to Danny's granddaughter, Remi Granger, who was an investigative reporter for one of the New Orleans TV stations.

"She's doing a piece on the murder tonight at ten."

"Really? What a coincidence."

"You haven't seen the promos for it? Channel Seven has been airing those all week."

"No, I guess not. I've been concentrating on writing since I have a quiet house. It's still a strange coincidence. But why air this now?"

"It will be twenty years ago this week since Melanie's murder. Remi told me she went to Mobile to speak with Tracy Lassiter. There will be an interview with her on air tonight."

"I'll be sure to watch. But first tell me what you know about the murder and the infamous ruby."

Rachel leaned back in her chair and appeared thoughtful for a long moment. "I remember when Danny worked on Melanie's case. Back then, Allemand Parish autopsies were carried out by Orleans Parish because we had no forensic pathologist on staff at the coroner's office here. Her death was ruled a homicide. She'd been shot."

"No suspects?"

She shook her head. "Every person of interest was eliminated. The case went cold."

"Do you think there's a chance the case might be reopened?"

"Danny would love to have it reopened. He can't stand to have any case go cold, especially a murder like this one."

"Okay, now what's the story on the ruby?"

"This is the way I heard it." She paused to take a sip of coffee. "Back in the nineteen-twenties, Edmund Haydel had a large multinational business with operations all over the world, including locations in Southeast Asia. It became too big for him to handle, so he sent his son Charles over to Burma to deal with the British. While Charles was living in Rangoon, he met and married the daughter of British missionaries. Her name was Harriet...don't remember her maiden name. Oh, yes, Blakewell..."

My writer's imagination fleshed out the details in my head as she relayed the story.

Rangoon, British Burma
March, 1924

The old ceiling fan only circulated hot air. Every once in a while, a breeze blew through the open windows and gave a small amount of relief from the oppressive heat and humidity.

Charles Haydel mopped his forehead with a white handkerchief. March and April were two of the hottest months of the year in Burma. He was ready to leave the jungles and head back home to Louisiana. Even with similar climates, Baton Rouge and New Orleans provided better accommodations, more graciousness, plus delicious food. In fact, even Allemand Parish had better lodgings and a higher degree of gentility.

The small amount of civility in Rangoon came from the British. However, most of the time they were snobbish and rude to anyone who wasn't their own people.

The weather wasn't the only problem in Burma these days. Riots by Burmese natives protesting British rule happened daily. The main dispute seemed to be the Brits' refusal to remove their shoes when entering a temple and other such cultural differences the Burmese found offensive. A few of the riots had turned deadly.

Come to think of it, there were only three Brits he found enjoyable, soon to be five. Believe it or not, he enjoyed being around his in-laws, John and Mary Blakewell. He laughed quietly. Two of those five would be half-British.

He glanced at his sleeping wife Harriet, who was eight months pregnant with twins. She had been ordered by her doctor to have complete bedrest until she delivered the babies.

As soon as she and the twins were able to travel, they would be leaving this dangerous place. The Blakewells were also considering leaving, although it was doubtful they would leave their mission and the people they had shepherded to Christianity.

Charles felt restless. His anxiety about what could be a risky delivery for Harriet, and concern about their chances of leaving the country before the turmoil turned into full-scale rebellion made him wish they could leave immediately. Not a single Anglo, neither British nor American, would be safe if more serious rioting took place.

He rose from his chair and walked over to the tall chest of drawers on the other side of the room. From the first drawer, he removed a blue velvet pouch and clutched it firmly in his right hand.

Emptying the bag into his other hand, he gazed at the largest and most beautiful ruby he'd ever seen. His mother had worn stunning jewelry, including a necklace of rubies and diamonds. But for some reason, this particular stone took his breath away.

Charles frowned, remembering an incident when he'd first brought the ruby home. He had been admiring the jewel in the hallway when a servant, an old Burmese woman, walked toward Harriet's bedroom to bring tea.

She dropped the tea tray, sending teapot and dishes crashing to the floor. "Nat is angry," she screamed. "Those who keep this ruby and their family will be cursed. It was stolen from a shrine."

Nat was a word in a local tribe's language that referred to a spirit or a god who guarded treasure. She had shouted the god's name, which Charles didn't quite catch. Even as long as he'd been in country, he had yet to master the language.

At the time, he dismissed her words as native superstition. How she knew the piece had been stolen from a shrine was a mystery to him. He had suspected the man who offered him the gem had lied about how he came into possession of it, but the ruby mesmerized him. He shook his head and again rejected any notion of a curse.

Even though he and his family would not be able to leave for six or eight months, he still needed to plan their journey back to the States. He replaced the ruby in its pouch and returned it to the drawer. Blowing a kiss in the direction of his sleeping wife as he left the room, Charles headed downstairs to his study to begin organizing all the paperwork required for their departure. A decision to have two of their Burmese servants accompany them home also had to be made.

Three

I widened my eyes. "Wow, that's quite the story." Never mind that I may have embellished the details somewhat in my imagination.

"I must admit to my fascination with the murder, but like you, more so about the ruby and the idea of a curse," Rachel said. "You may recall I have a degree in anthropology with an emphasis on folk legends, myths, and rituals."

"Oh yes, I remember now. You helped decipher the contents of the gris gris bag found on the two bodies during Mardi Gras season years ago." I cringed at the thought. Another event I didn't care to recall.

As if she sensed my discomfort, Rachel quickly added, "When Danny was working on this case, I delved into all I could find on the ruby, along with a lot of the reports about the murder itself."

"Did Danny have any suspects for Melanie's murder? I mean a person who his gut told him had committed it?"

"He strongly suspected her ex-husband Brett Lassiter, but he supposedly had an alibi. Whoever killed her must have stolen the ruby, because the stone and her killer simply disappeared from the face of the earth." Rachel lifted her hands, palms up. "I know people don't simply disappear. However, it's been almost twenty years. He or she could be anywhere in the world. Or, the killer could be dead by now."

"Is Brett Lassiter still alive?"

Rachel shrugged. "As far as anyone knows. No one that I know of has heard from him in ages. Tracy may have been in contact with him. Or Danny may have information on his whereabouts."

"By the way, where is Danny?"

"Down at the sheriff's office." She took the last swallow of her coffee and pushed the empty cup to the side. "Not long before you came over, Ronnie called and asked if he could meet with him. There was something he wanted to discuss."

I frowned. "Hopefully, the matter Ronnie wanted to talk to him about didn't involve me."

She looked surprised. "Why would it?"

I explained about my visit to the old cemetery and my interaction with Ronnie when he'd caught me leaving the property. I didn't mention my encounter with the graffiti artist.

"You are being paranoid. From your conversation with him, I can't see any reason why he would call Danny all the way down to city hall merely to tell him to keep you away from posted property."

I gave a long sigh. "I suppose you're right, but law enforcement always seems to rush to judgment about my actions. In this case, I didn't even discover a dead body," I added, trying to discourage any idea that I might be considering a murder investigation. Rachel would never think such a thing of me. Ha. Ha.

She gave a low chuckle. "It's kind of strange. All those other times when you discovered a murder victim, you weren't trespassing or someplace you shouldn't have been." She eyed me for a long moment. "You are thinking about delving into Melanie's murder, aren't you?"

Before I could respond, Danny came into the kitchen through the carport door. We had been so engrossed in our conversation, neither Rachel nor I had heard him drive up. Apparently we had guilty looks on our faces because he stopped short. "What kind of foolishness are you two drumming up?"

"Not a thing," Rachel said. "We were discussing Susan's visit to the Haydel-LeBlanc cemetery and, also, Melanie's murder."

Danny had a strange expression on his face, a combination of surprise and suspicion. "Ronnie told me about your visit," he said. "And your run-in with the guy who seems to think he's Michelangelo."

To cover my guilt for not being completely honest with Rachel, I pointed a finger at her. "Didn't I tell you? Ronnie probably asked Danny to keep me from trespassing on posted property or suddenly deciding to open a cold case investigation on my own."

Rachel glared at me. "You did not tell me about the aforementioned incident with 'Michelangelo.' What's that all about?"

Danny waved his hands to stop any further discussion. "Her explanation can wait until later."

He fixed me with a steely look. "As a matter of fact, he did not ask me to curtail your activities. Tell me this. Did you by some chance contact Tracy Lassiter after you left the cemetery?"

His question caught me by surprise. "I thought about calling her, but any contact I'd have with her right now would be an invasion of privacy."

He raised his eyebrows. "Right now?"

I leaned back in my chair. "Bad choice of words." I explained once again how I discovered the article about Melanie's death and the ruby. "You know how my mind works. I got caught up in the story and wanted to find out more. I couldn't very well call her out of the blue and start asking questions about her mother's murder. I didn't know about Remi's investigative piece until Rachel told me."

Danny pulled a chair away from the table and sat. He didn't say anything for a long moment. "You and Ms. Lassiter must be on the same wavelength."

I couldn't imagine why he would make such a statement. I glanced at Rachel and could tell by her expression the same thought had occurred to her.

"After Ronnie went in with a couple of deputies to check the place out, he contacted Tracy about the lock on the gate being broken. He located the graffiti painted on the tombstone of Charles Haydel, as you'd reported. Ronnie believes it's possible the man you encountered was hanging around when you walked up."

"He must have arrived only a short time before me." The thought gave me a chill, considering Ronnie's warning about returning by myself. "What does that have to do with Tracy Lassiter and me being of the same mind?"

"When Ronnie talked to Tracy to give her the details of the incident, she asked him if it was possible to reopen her mother's case. She mentioned Remi's piece that will air tonight. That's why he wanted to talk to me. He asked if I would reopen this cold case."

"And of course, you told him yes," Rachel said. I couldn't tell whether she was happy about this new development or not.

"You bet your life I did. In fact, I have three boxes of reports and other related items out in my truck." Danny appeared thoughtful for a short moment. "Melanie's killer was the only perpetrator my department didn't bring to justice during my time as sheriff. I'm going to do everything in my power to do that this time."

Mobile, Alabama

Tracy Lassiter's gaze moved to a folder sitting atop her desk. She could repeat from memory the info on all those photos, the death certificates for her mother and other ancestors who'd died under so-called suspicious circumstances, and the various police reports. The family story of how her great-great grandfather obtained the ruby alleged to curse its owners had become etched in her mind.

Her mother's death remained in the back of her mind every day. Discovering her body had almost destroyed Tracy. Yet there was a missing piece. A scene from that night she couldn't remember. Probably her use of pot and drinking too much made her forget part of what had happened after she'd discovered the body.

She absentmindedly tossed a pair of capri pants and a blouse into the suitcase lying open on her bed. Giving a sigh, she removed the items and folded them properly. She couldn't arrive in Allemand Parish with a bunch of wrinkled clothes. She could always buy new ones.

Buying new outfits wouldn't present a financial problem for her with the sizable inheritance she'd been left by her mother. For reasons beyond her comprehension, she still felt the need to live up to her mother's reputation as a classy dresser. What a joke. Her taste in clothing would never come close to her mother's. Melanie LeBlanc Lassiter may not have been a great mother, or a great person for that matter, but she didn't deserve to be brutally murdered.

As a sixteen-year-old at the time of the murder, Tracy had had no choice about staying in Allemand Parish. Her Lassiter grandmother had taken her away to their home in Mobile.

Well, she wasn't a teenager any longer. Grandma Lassiter had passed away years ago. This time around, she intended to stay in Cypress Lake until she got results: either closure or justice...or both.

As far as the ruby was concerned, Tracy hoped it would never be located. She and her family had been living with the ruby's cloud looming over them for too many years.

Four

I couldn't believe Danny allowed Rachel and me to look at the case files with him. He probably only wanted Rachel's thoughts about the myth concerning the ruby, but hey, I got to dig into this right along with them.

In my mind, I pushed aside my current work in progress and decided to concentrate on this story. This was a local mystery, too close to home to be ignored. To top it off, the original Louisiana purchaser of the jewel was the father of twins. How could I disregard a story dealing with a multiple birth? I have a twin brother and my two children are twins.

"Do you know if Tracy Lassiter will be coming back to Cypress Lake now that her mother's murder case is being reopened?" I asked.

"I believe so," Danny replied. "Ronnie mentioned she indicated she wanted to be here for the investigation. I may need to interview her again about what she may have witnessed." He thumbed through a few pages in the file. "She may not know a whole lot. As I recall, she had been out partying with a group of teenagers the night of the murder and arrived home to discover the body."

"Discovering a body is bad enough, but with the victim being a parent, it must have been extremely traumatic for a teenager," I said. "How old was she? About fifteen or sixteen?"

"Sixteen," Rachel answered. "Danny makes it sound like she had gone bar hopping. The kids she was with were attending a school prom."

He tilted his head slightly, giving her a superior look. "They also hung out at a couple of after-parties following the prom. You know what most of those evolve into."

Could she have killed her mother? "I hate to ask...was Tracy ever considered a suspect?"

"I did consider her a suspect at first," Danny said, looking pensive. "Many others in local law enforcement also believed she was a viable suspect because of a few run-ins between her and her mother."

"Why did you end up believing in her innocence?"

"Because she had rock-solid alibis from the school and the two other parties she attended."

I decided to play devil's advocate. "Couldn't all those people who alibied her have been drunk or stoned and therefore unreliable?"

He arched a brow. "Are you training to become a prosecutor?"

I laughed. "No, but I'm sure the DA would've brought that up."

"Yeah, you're right. John Vincent held the office back then. He thought she was a viable suspect. For a while, I was overruled on my decision to drop her from the suspect list. I, along with everyone else on scene, knew she'd been drinking. Her clothes smelled like weed."

My mouth gaped open. "Then why on earth did you not consider her a suspect?"

"Tracy was really in bad shape and in no condition to have killed her mother, who was shot four times, plus she'd suffered a severe beating prior. The official time of death confirmed Melanie had been killed around the time Tracy arrived to discover the body. Also, she didn't have blood on her clothes nor did she have gunshot residue on her body. If she would have been sober and in better shape, the story might have ended there. She might have been my main suspect, for a while at least."

"Sounds reasonable, but couldn't she have had one of her friends do the job for her?"

"That's possible, but no suspect ever came up." He frowned. "There's a number of old timers who still believe she's guilty."

"What about those other so-called mysterious deaths in the family? I mean the deaths that local legend attributes to the curse of the ruby." I thought Danny might laugh at the idea of a jewel's being cursed. Surprisingly, he didn't.

"I don't believe in curses or hexes being placed on people, or evil spirits hurting or killing humans," he said, "but a lot of people around here believe in Voodoo and other similar belief systems. There are people who are certain Big Foot is real. And you know the stories about Rougaroo, the werewolf of the swamp."

"Oh yes, and then there's putting the gris gris on someone," I said. "But back to these deaths. How did those family members die?"

He turned to Rachel. "I don't remember when the first one occurred, but it seems like Charles Haydel died sometime in the nineteen-thirties."

Rachel agreed. "He supposedly fell off the second story balcony of his house. Broke his neck, I believe."

"His death was ruled an accident," Danny continued. "There wasn't any evidence to prove otherwise. The report indicated witnesses all said he was pretty drunk."

"I suppose back then there wasn't a lot of forensic work that could be done," I mused.

"No, there wasn't, but I've studied the report in depth and I didn't see anything in the file to show Haydel's death was other than accidental." He glanced at Rachel before turning to me. "I'm only interested in solving Melanie LeBlanc's murder. All those other deaths in that family were not considered suspicious in any way by anybody except superstitious neighbors and household staff."

"In other words, I should keep my nose out," I said with a clipped tone.

He shook his head. "You can look into them if you'd like, but I'm certain you won't find anything incriminating or questionable in

Haydel's death or any of the others. As I recall, the two other deaths included a traffic accident and a death during childbirth."

I could probably turn either one of those incidents into great plot twists in my novel if he turned out to be correct. "Will you let me have a copy of Charles Haydel's accident report?"

He stared at me for a long moment. "I tell you what. I'll make copies of his report for you. You can investigate to your heart's content."

"Great." I knew he was trying to pacify me so I would stay out of his hair during his investigation. I let it go without further comment. One never knew what might have been missed the first or even the second time around.

"The traffic accident involved a hit and run," Rachel said. "Anne LeBlanc, Melanie's mother, was killed out on Richard Road late one night. The sheriff at that time believed the person who hit her was most likely drunk and didn't want to be arrested."

"How long ago did this happen?"

"Some time in the nineteen-seventies," Danny said. "That file is also in here with all the information about Melanie's murder. I'll even make you a copy of that one."

A hit and run made another interesting scenario. Maybe the incident wasn't an accident. Someone could have hit her on purpose.

Danny rose and picked up two of the file boxes. "I'm going to my office to do some serious work on these files. I'll make you a copy of Haydel's report and the hit and run, Susan. I'll bring them out in a few minutes."

He returned later for the third box and removed it to his office.

I waited until he'd disappeared into the other room the final time before speaking. "He certainly is anxious to keep me out of his investigation. I can't believe he agreed to give me access to those other deaths, although I'm sure the reason he did is because he firmly believes there's no murder involved."

Rachel gave a low chuckle. "True, but you know what happens when you start investigating. You end up in a lot of trouble." She paused for a second or two. "Actually, I'm kind of interested in those two incidents myself. The childbirth death could possibly be murder, but it's not very probable."

"I agree with you on that one. The others are more likely to be homicide."

"Now, tell me about the incident at the cemetery," Rachel said with the firmness of a parent questioning a teenager about some infraction.

Five

After I finished retelling my cemetery story, Rachel and I studied the report for Charles Haydel's death for quite some time, finding nothing suspicious or interesting in it. Danny might be correct in his conclusion concerning the cases, at least this one.

Haydel appeared to witnesses to be extremely intoxicated on the evening of his death. Others told the sheriff that Charles had been depressed for months since the death of his young daughter. Some suggested he may have committed suicide by jumping. All indications were that he'd lost his balance and fallen off the balcony. His death was ruled an accident.

The hit-and-run report appeared to be much of the same. According to the record, Anne was driving south on Richard Road late one night. Damage to the driver's side indicated her car had been hit by a passing car, forcing her to lose control of the vehicle. She ended up in a ditch on the side of the road. The accident wasn't discovered until one the next morning, about two hours after her time of death was confirmed.

"The driver of the other vehicle failed to stop, even though it was not likely said driver did not realize he or she had struck another

vehicle," the responding deputy wrote. "*Unless the driver was so drunk, he or she was not aware of their surroundings.*"

"I presume that's how they decided the hit-and-run driver left the scene because he didn't want to be caught," I said. "The time of the accident seems odd. What was Anne doing alone at that time of night?"

"Makes you wonder, doesn't it?" Rachel's voice held a hint of sarcasm.

"Do you think our DWI suspect was someone high up in Allemand Parish's social hierarchy, who might have paid to get out of the mess?"

"Anything is possible around here. Especially with who happened to be sheriff at the time."

"Who was the sheriff then?"

"Rodney Hebert. Everybody called him Gun. He was Tank Hebert's older brother."

I groaned. "Is Gun still alive?"

Rachel made a face. "Yes, he is. He's up in his nineties, living in a nursing home. I don't know how lucid he is, but I would not want to find out."

"Sounds like a real nice guy. Much like his younger brother." I thought for a moment. "He must have been a lot older than Tank."

"Gun was the oldest of fourteen kids; Tank was the youngest."

Tank Hebert was the Cypress Lake chief of police before my late husband Jim took over the position. Today he's in prison for the attempted murder of Megan Whitehall, now LaGrange—my brother Steven's second wife.

Disappointed with the results of our review of those two documents, I leaned back in the chair and gave a sigh. "I guess Danny was correct in his assessment about the other family deaths."

"I feel kind of let down myself," Rachel admitted.

At that moment, Danny returned to the kitchen holding a piece of paper in his hand. He had a sheepish expression on his face. "Susan, you may be right about at least one of these deaths."

I sat up straight. "Which one?"

"The hit and run," he said. "Here's why." He displayed the paper he held. "This is an invoice from the garage where Anne's car was towed. I found it folded up and mixed in with other papers at the back of the folder. This is one of those files that has not yet been saved to the computer system, which is why this note hadn't been discovered yet."

Rachel and I both expressed shock at the same time, after reading the note.

"The mechanic discovered the brake lines on her car had been cut?" My question was rhetorical.

"This is unreal," Rachel said. "I don't understand why no one saw this, or if they did, tucked it away."

"My thoughts exactly. Why didn't anyone follow up on this?" I asked, not really expecting a logical answer.

"I have an idea," Danny said, a frown wrinkling his brow. "There's also another invoice without mention of the brake lines placed up front where anyone glancing through the file would see that one. I intend to include this in my review.

"At the time that I conducted my investigation on Melanie's murder, a family member asked...no...demanded that I look into the other deaths," he continued. "This file could not be located. When Ronnie requested files on all the other deaths to give to me, an eagle-eyed deputy discovered it misfiled in the many boxes of records that were scheduled to be put on computer."

"Bravo for him," I said.

"You ladies will be happy to know the deputy who located the file was a female," he said. "I hope Ronnie puts her in for a promotion."

"Me, too. An even bigger bravo for her." A thought occurred to me. "Is it possible there was no hit and run and Anne's murder was covered up?"

"Absolutely," Danny said.

Six

Tuesday, July 15

Remi's interview with Tracy Lassiter on last night's news show had portrayed the public image of the Haydel, Richard, and LeBlanc families to be quite different from their private reality, which is not unusual with people who are wealthy. Of course, this could be true with any family, middle class or lower.

Remi's talent for subtlety in depicting her subject matter without being tabloid-ish had allowed the viewers to come to the same conclusion about the individuals under her microscope as her investigation was suggesting.

I came away with this impression: The men were all heavy drinkers and big socializers, all the way down the line to Carl LeBlanc and Brett Lassiter. It wouldn't have surprised me if those two had numerous mistresses on the side. Charles Haydel appeared to be the only man who'd remained faithful to his wife, but then he may have kept his affairs totally under wraps. The wives all enjoyed spending money and living in the lap of luxury.

Tracy admitted she hadn't had a good relationship with her mother, Melanie. I could see why some law enforcement people might consider her a suspect, but I felt she was telling the truth about not being involved. Tracy also mentioned the other family deaths, which the household staff believed to have been brought on by the ruby's curse.

I mulled over Remi's piece along with the police report of the so-called hit-and-run incident while I sipped my morning coffee. Anne LeBlanc had been killed in May of 1974. The Vietnam War was still raging and people were protesting it. What else was going on in the world?

Better question…what had been happening in Allemand Parish during the seventies and who might have wanted Anne dead? The obituary listed her husband Carl as a survivor. Maybe he'd wanted to be free of his wife. Did he kill Anne because of one affair in particular? A sexual affair was a common motive for murder of a spouse. But so was gaining money from a life insurance policy, or not wanting to pay alimony in a divorce settlement.

Rachel had indicated the sheriff may have played a hand in allowing Anne's death to be reported as an accident instead of murder. Paid off by someone?

A similar scene of corruption had caused Jim's death. Starting from the mayor, a childhood friend of his, on down to the coroner and through some CLPD officers and a few deputies who were all involved in a drug smuggling operation.

Voices from outside the Marchands' house drew my attention away from murder. A few minutes later, I heard a knock at the kitchen door. I figured my visitor was Rachel, but I was wrong. Remi Granger greeted me when I opened the door.

"Hey, Susan, are you busy right now?"

"No, I was lounging about mulling over your interview with Tracy and some other info we discovered yesterday. Come on in and have a seat."

She sat on the sofa next to the chair I refer to as my "security blanket chair," a comfortable overstuffed wingback. "By we, if you mean Gramps and Rachel, they told me about all the interesting info hidden away in the file."

"I'll bet they swore you to secrecy. I had to take the oath of silence."

"Naturally, they did. But I'm anxious to investigate further. I figured since you knew the story and were most likely under the same restrictions, you and I could discuss the details."

"Is it a coincidence you're here in town today or were you planning all along to do more investigating? The whole story is pretty fascinating."

"Actually, I received a call from Tracy last night. She drove in from Mobile yesterday and wanted me to meet her for coffee at the Court House Café." She hesitated a short moment. "She asked me if you would join us."

I did a double take. "Me? Why me?"

"She said the sheriff told her about your encounter with the graffiti artist and she wanted to know everything you saw."

"I have pictures on my cell of the graffiti and the man as he was running away. I vaguely recall what his face looked like. I was too busy dodging spray paint."

"So, will you join us?" She eyed me expectantly.

"Sure, why not?" I pursed my lips. "I'm concerned about what can be revealed to Tracy. I don't want to blurt out something she is better off not knowing."

"Obviously Danny doesn't want to reveal the statement from the garage about the brake line cut on her grandmother's car yet. He wants to give her the information himself when he thinks the time is right. She does have a meeting scheduled with him later this morning. I think we should not mention anything at all about Anne LeBlanc's death. If she brings up the subject, we'll claim ignorance about any clues and tell her she'll have to speak to Danny about any concerns." She paused for a split second. "Besides, he's more interested in Melanie's murder. He said in so many words that he'd dig into Anne LeBlanc's death after he'd solved Melanie's.

"Sounds like a plan," I said. "Why don't I meet you there? I have a few errands to run before our meeting. I won't be long."

"Okay, I'll see you in a little bit."

I watched her walk across the driveway and get into her car. I didn't really have any errands to run. Guess I was stalling.

The café is located directly across the street from city hall, which also houses the Cypress Lake Police Department and the Allemand Parish Sheriff's Office. Going to the Court House Café would bring back unpleasant memories.

Seven

I took a long look around inside the café without seeing the big picture. I was too busy trying to block from my mind the moment nearly two years ago when I realized who had killed Jim. On that day, I had an unexpected meeting with the former mayor's wife who unknowingly provided the information. Coincidently, her name happened to be Tracy. Another reminder.

Spotting Remi and Tracy Lassiter seated in a booth near the window, I took a deep breath and walked toward them. After my introduction to Tracy, I waved to the waitress to take my order.

"I'll have a cup of coffee and a sweet roll," I told her. She scribbled the order on her pad and walked off toward the kitchen.

Tracy tilted her head to the side. "Susan, I understand you were more or less accosted by the man who painted graffiti on my great-great-grandfather's tomb."

"I guess you could say that. But I was trespassing at the time."

She waved off my admission. "I'm not worried about you trespassing. Can you describe this guy?"

"I can only give my impression because I was trying to avoid being hit with black spray paint. I remember he appeared young, like late teens or early twenties, and something about his face seemed vaguely Asian. He was definitely in shape, able to sprint away and leap over the fence at the rear of the cemetery with ease." I reached in my purse and pulled out my cell phone. "Here, I'll show you some pictures I snapped. The one of him is a shot running away, so you can't see his face."

I keyed up the photos and handed her the phone. She studied the photo of the young man for a long moment.

"Do you recognize him?" Remi asked.

"Something about his gait seems familiar, but I can't place him. I can't imagine why he would seem familiar. I can't even see his face. It's been at least four years since I've been back to Allemand Parish for legal business concerning the property. He's also a lot younger than me." She handed the phone back. "The sheriff told me you had given him photos of the guy and the graffiti he left, but Sheriff Hart didn't provide them to me. Will you send them to my phone?"

"Sure, I'd be happy to."

At that moment, the waitress delivered my coffee and sweet roll to the table and refilled the cups of the other two women. After she left, I got Tracy's phone number and sent the photos to her cell.

Her phone dinged. "I got them. Thanks." She frowned. "The graffiti is disturbing." She looked up and moved her gaze from me to Remi and back. "This guy seems too young to know about the ruby."

"I wondered about that myself," I said. "Could he be a relative, like a great-grandson or nephew of one of your family members?"

Tracy looked thoughtful as she twirled a strand of her long dark hair with one finger. "It's a possibility, I suppose, but I'm at a loss as to who that might be. As far as I know, I'm the only one left in the direct line. Of course, there could be fourth or fifth cousins still living in the area. Names like LeBlanc, Richard, and Haydel are prevalent around here."

"People who feel neglected or jealous of other family members often murder for those reasons," Remi said. "This might be a subject to bring up with Danny this morning when y'all meet. Try making a list of every family member you can recall, starting with your great-grandfather, Charles Haydel."

She perked up. "My maternal grandmother had the family tree drawn up by a professional genealogist and published the information in a book. I received the book with all of Mom's things after her murder. I wasn't interested in old history at the time, but I kept it. If Danny thinks the idea has merit, I'll need to make a quick trip back to Mobile."

I figuratively bit my tongue to keep from revealing the cut brake line on her grandmother Anne LeBlanc's car, but resigned myself to the idea Danny should tell her if he believed the information is important to his case.

"Even if he doesn't think so, I say go get the book anyway," I said. "Cops don't always think civilians know a lot about solving a murder. Believe me, I can vouch for that."

Tracy smiled. "I've heard about some of your adventures."

~ * ~

He covertly watched the women seated in the booth across the room from his table. If they had been any other three females, he wouldn't have paid attention to them except to admire their good looks. This little meeting did not bode well for him and the others.

Remi Granger, the investigative reporter, had already proved her interest in the newly opened cold case. In addition to discussing Melanie's murder, her interview with Tracy Lassiter last night revealed information long forgotten by the public.

The so-called mysterious deaths of other family members and that stupid business about the ruby being associated with a curse on whoever owned the jewel would get the tabloids buzzing for sure. The family's way of life cursed them, not the jewel.

He smiled to himself. Making the whole family believe in the curse had started with his great-grandmother and after her story passed down to him, certainly made for a lot of amusement in his otherwise dull life. Too bad his grandfather and his father couldn't have been there to see the Haydel clan's disarray years ago.

Susan Foret nosing around only meant trouble for him. She was known for investigating murders on her own. With her connection to law enforcement and her PI boyfriend, she would have access to a lot of info ordinary people wouldn't have.

And then there was Tracy herself. She made it clear she intended to make sure her mother's killer was caught and punished.

He could not allow them to stop him and the group from getting retribution.

Eight

I usually check out all the patrons upon entering a restaurant or café. Observing them helps make for more realistic fictional characters. Today I hadn't noticed anyone who looked suspicious in the Court House Café until I left the place. I had tunnel vision, along with blinders, in order to keep my mind clear of bad memories.

The customers included two women seated at a table close to the wall, a man with gray hair who had a newspaper spread out on his table, and three uniformed city police officers. I didn't recognize any of them. After almost two years since Jim's murder, there must be pretty close to a whole new crew of officers in both the sheriff's office and the city police department.

None of the customers present appeared to pose any kind of threat or even seemed interesting. Maybe if I'd had a chance to observe them longer, I would have discovered some noteworthy trait or physical characteristic on which I could base a character...or I might have sensed something suspicious about who they were in real life.

Remi, Tracy, and I stood outside the café a few feet away from the entrance for a short time chatting and vowing to meet again soon. I parted company with them and started walking toward my car, which was parked in the opposite direction of theirs.

I glanced toward the café entrance as I walked past. A man with gray hair stood outside holding what appeared to be a cell phone in his hand, a newspaper tucked under his arm. Nothing unusual about that. I recognized him as the man seated at a table reading the newspaper.

I nodded to him and gave a friendly smile. He returned the nod, but the look he gave me when our eyes met felt creepy. I couldn't put my finger on why I found him disturbing. He broke eye contact and began keying in a number on his cell phone.

Nothing about his physical appearance seemed out of place. He seemed to be in his late fifties or early sixties, nice-looking, and neatly dressed. Why would he give me the creeps?

If my past experiences are any example of how life goes for me, he's most likely one of those people who has some connection to the incident I happen to be investigating.

Investigating? Wow, I guess I should get a PI license even if it means having a gun. There are gun cases to keep weapons under lock and key. I wouldn't need to carry a gun around with me all the time. If I'm going to investigate, I might as well do it somewhat legally.

But that's a project for another time. Maybe after Josh returns from his seminar, he can help me with everything that's involved. Or maybe I should leave well enough alone. Forget having a PI license and a gun.

I continued to my car and slipped into what felt like an oven. The seats, steering wheel, and everything metal or plastic stung any exposed skin. I quickly started the car and turned the air conditioner on full blast. As I pulled out of the parking lot, I glanced toward the café. The man was no longer in sight. He must have gone back inside. He couldn't possibly have disappeared so quickly. Or could he?

I drove past the café searching for any escape route he could have taken on foot. *Listen to me. I'm jumping to a lot of conclusions.* His car could have been two feet away. But then I remembered another incident about three years ago that happened right in front of city hall, across the street. My sister-in-law Megan was shot as she'd exited the building after meeting with Jim and Danny. Figuring out who shot her took weeks, but eventually the shooter, Tank Hebert, was caught and convicted.

My heart jumped. Tracy had an appointment with Danny for eleven this morning at city hall. Supposedly lightning doesn't strike twice in the same place. I don't know about that.

I pulled over into a parking spot along the curb and picked up my cell phone. Danny wouldn't be happy to hear from me, especially with some crazy idea about the possibility of Tracy's getting shot. My conversation with Danny went as I expected.

"You believe Tracy might be in danger because you're having flashbacks of Megan's getting shot?" he said. "I think your imagination is working overtime."

"Please keep my warning in mind. Think about it."

He gave an audible sigh. "Okay, if it'll make you feel better, I'll walk her out to her car when we finish our interview."

"Thank you. I hope I'm wrong."

I ended the call and decided to drive to Lake Front Park, an area on the shore of Lake Cypress. I've always enjoyed hearing water lap against the pier and viewing the row of cypress trees that marked the end of Allemand Bayou as it flowed into the lake. The scene was so peaceful.

It seemed everyone in town had the same idea. There were too many people there. I opted to go home, but I took a longer route, stalling for time. Anything to avoid the empty house. A stop at Walmart, browsing and doing some early school shopping for the twins, took up more time.

I checked my watch as I walked out of the store. Wow, I didn't realize I'd been in there for over an hour. I figured if I wanted to further delay my arrival home, I'd have to drive all the way to New Orleans. I had no intention of going to NOLA.

Anxiety rose inside me as I pulled into my driveway. At first, I had thought the peace and quiet in the house with everyone being gone would be great for working on my novel. Although I had gotten a good bit of the story completed, I'd discovered for the most part the silence didn't help my concentration. I had to turn a radio on, something

I'd never done when writing. Knowing my kids weren't nearby was a major distraction.

I didn't want to go inside to an empty house, so I walked across the yard and knocked on Rachel's door. After a few minutes she answered and motioned me inside.

"You want some coffee?" she asked.

I shook my head. "I've had enough caffeine for a while."

"Come sit at the table," she said. "Remi told me about your meeting with her and Tracy."

"Is she here?"

"Not at the moment. In fact, you missed her by about five minutes. I'm surprised you didn't see her leaving. She got a phone call and took off without saying where she was going." Her brow wrinkled. "I have the feeling something is wrong. I mean, not like breaking news, but something more personal."

I eyed her with caution. "Personal to her or to you?"

"Maybe both." She changed the subject. "Tell me about the meeting."

"The last time I went to the Court House Café, the identity of Jim's killer came to me. There was also another bad memory involving that place and city hall. It's where Megan was shot when she came out of the building after her interview with Jim and Danny. I had a few flashbacks."

She reached out and patted my arm. "I can imagine you would."

"I felt as if there might be a repeat with Tracy," I said. "I phoned Danny and..."

The sound of a car turning into the driveway interrupted my disclosure. Rachel sat up straight.

Several car doors slammed. I exchanged a curious look with her. We both rose and went to the window. Ronnie Hart had exited his marked unit and was going around to the passenger side. Someone had driven Danny's truck and parked it in front of the house. Remi pulled up in my driveway to keep from blocking Ronnie's vehicle.

Rachel took a deep breath. "Danny's been hurt." She rushed out the door with me right behind her.

He had a bandage and sling on his right arm and was walking with a stiffness that suggested he might have taken a fall. But I had the feeling his injuries were not exclusively from a fall. He'd been shot. With Remi hovering on one side and Ronnie on the other, he met Rachel halfway to the door.

"What happened?" Rachel cried. "How bad are you hurt?"

He shook his head. "We can discuss all that in a minute. Let me get inside first."

"I'll get his medication out of the car," Ronnie said. He strolled back over to the passenger side of his unit and reached in, removing a plastic bag bearing a local drug store's red logo.

We all went back inside and gathered in the den. Danny sat in his recliner with help from Rachel. Remi and I slipped onto the sofa while Ronnie perched on its arm.

I'm sure Rachel was even more anxious than I was to hear what had happened. She pulled one of the dining room chairs next to the recliner.

Danny eyed me for a long moment with a hard stare. An uncomfortable feeling made my stomach clench. I had no idea why he was giving me such a look.

"In the future I will need to start taking your hunches a little more seriously," he said, slurring his words slightly. "I started to question your intuition about Tracy's being in danger. But I decided to walk her out after we'd finished our talk as I told you I would, even though I didn't put much stock in anything happening. I was wrong."

"Someone shot at you and Tracy?" Rachel asked.

He grimaced. "He…or she, fired two shots in close succession. The first one hit the concrete walkway at our feet. I pushed Tracy out of the way in time for the second shot to hit me in the arm."

Ronnie spoke up as if in answer to my unspoken question. "Tracy only has a few bumps and bruises. She's pretty shook up."

I squeezed my eyes shut and let out a sigh. "When I phoned you, I was hoping my imagination really was running amok."

"You didn't explain what brought on the idea that Tracy would be in danger," Danny said. "There's got to be more to this than your flashback about Megan's shooting."

I explained how a man who had been in the café acted after we went outside. "He gave me an uneasy feeling because he seemed to be concentrating on us."

"Could he simply have been admiring three good-looking women?" Ronnie asked.

I made a face. "Women know when a man is admiring them or if he's creepy and has something else in mind."

"Describe him."

"In his late fifties or early sixties with gray hair. Neatly dressed, dark trousers, light-colored polo shirt."

"So he didn't look like a homeless person," Ronnie said.

"Dressing nicely doesn't make him less creepy." His questions irritated me. I found his tone condescending.

Rachel hovered around Danny, who looked as if he were about to fall asleep. "Did the doctor give you something for pain before you left the ER?"

He mumbled something I couldn't catch. Rachel glanced at Ronnie. "I believe we need to cut this short." I had the same thought.

"I agree," he said. "Do you need help getting him into bed?"

"No, for the time being he's okay. Later, if I decide to move him, I'll have help." She glanced at Remi and me.

"Count on it," I said. *And count on me to find out who tried to kill Tracy and/or Danny and why.*

Nine

I walked outside with Ronnie, hoping he would give me more details about the incident. "Did y'all locate any evidence of where the shooter stood?"

He shook his head. "We haven't found any empty cartridges so far. The shooter may have picked them up. I've got my deputies still combing the area." He pulled his cell phone from his pocket. "I need to check in with headquarters to see if anything turned up."

He walked a short distance away from me and turned his back. After completing his conversation, he returned to me. "Still nothing."

"When Danny pushed Tracy out of the way, did they both fall to the ground?"

He gave me a curious look. "Why do you want to know?"

"I guess that was a strange question," I said. "I'm trying to determine exactly how serious Danny's injuries are."

"Yes, he and Tracy both fell to the ground." He put his hand on my arm. "Don't worry. I can assure you he was given a full exam. No broken bones. The shot to his arm went straight through without causing much damage. We have located the slug. Any more questions?"

"No, that's all." I watched him drive away, and then started back inside. Maybe I wasn't giving Danny enough credit. I knew he kept in shape, but a gunshot wound and a hard fall to the ground might not be as easy for a seventy-year-old to recuperate from as for a younger person like Tracy.

Or...maybe I'm having flashbacks to Jim's death. I took a deep breath and assured myself that my father figure would be good as new sooner rather than later. Speaking of fathers, I think I'll give my real dad a call this evening. It's been a while since we talked.

While Danny snoozed away in his recliner, Rachel, Remi, and I sat at the kitchen table and discussed the latest event.

Rachel gave Remi a stern look. "Why didn't you tell me about Danny's injury when you received that phone call?"

"I didn't know how bad the situation was at the time. All Ronnie told me was that he had been shot and the wound wasn't serious. I didn't want you to get upset over something minor so I had to see for myself in case Ronnie was minimizing the seriousness." She reached over and took Rachel's hand. "Hope you're not mad at me."

Rachel gave a faint smile. "I'm not upset with you. Actually, it was probably better he told you. I might have fallen apart."

I gave her a skeptical look. "I can't imagine you being anything other than calmly taking charge of the situation."

"Exactly like you did," Remi said.

My cell phone rang. I checked the display and noted the time. One in the afternoon. "Hi, Josh. I didn't expect your call so early in the day."

"We heard about a shooting in Cypress Lake. What happened?"

"News travels fast. All the way to Baton Rouge. Danny was shot in the arm. He's at home. He's asleep now from the pain killer the ER doctor gave him, but he'll be okay in a day or two, if I know him."

"What happened? Do they know who shot him?" A trace of concern sounded in his voice, although I could tell he was trying to hide any note of uneasiness.

"The answer to your second question is no. The answer to the first one will take a while to explain. It's a long story."

"Tell me the basics. You can fill me in on the rest later."

"Danny had a meeting with Tracy Lassiter this morning. I know you don't know her, but anyway…" I relayed the rest of the story about how Danny had been wounded.

"Sounds like someone might have been aiming for the woman." I heard a male voice in the background. "Listen, I've got to go. I'll call you back later this evening and you can explain everything to me. Stay out of trouble." He laughed. "I doubt that's possible."

"*Moi*?" I teased, pointing a finger to my chest.

"Seriously, be careful."

"I will. Talk to you later." We ended the call. I turned back to Rachel and Remi who gave me surprised looks.

"My colleagues from other TV stations have the jump on me," Remi said, a frown wrinkling her brow. "And I'm right in the middle of the situation."

"Does that bother you?" I asked.

"What upsets me is how the story will be reported on the other stations."

"Remi, don't concern yourself about how the media outlets portray Cypress Lake or Allemand Parish," Rachel said. "I can't believe Josh heard about it in Baton Rouge. News sure travels fast when there's some violence."

Remi sighed. "I'll try not to worry about it."

"Josh probably heard about the shooting through some of the guys at the seminar. Most of them have law enforcement connections. I doubt the Baton Rouge stations would be interested."

Rachel glanced at the wall clock. "Now, I suggest we leave this discussion for the time being. I suddenly realized it's past lunch time. I have salad fixings and also ham or turkey slices if you two want sandwiches."

I figured her change of subject was to help divert our attention and hers from dwelling too much on Danny's wound. Could the shooter have been aiming for him? Or was Tracy the target? My bet, like Josh's, was on Tracy.

I forced my thoughts in another direction…food. Even though one doesn't usually think of salads and sandwiches as comfort food, I believe one's company furthers the process along.

~ * ~

He paced the floor in his home office, taking a few swipes through his hair with his hand. The assignment he'd given to his nephew was a terrible mistake, basically a knee-jerk reaction. Although at the time he'd thought the kid knew how to take care of business in a more covert manner. Shooting in such a public place had only brought more attention to them. Not only from the media, but law enforcement as well, with one of their own wounded. Next time there would be more planning involved. He would do the job himself. For now, it was best to lay low.

Ten

About three Josh called me back. He must really be worried. I wasn't expecting his call until later this evening. Leaving Rachel and Remi in the kitchen, I answered in the privacy of the Marchands' living room. I filled him in with the rest of the story, including the legend of the cursed ruby and the cut brake lines on Anne LeBlanc's car. I also told him about my adventure at the cemetery. He didn't say anything for a few moments.

"I gather you're intent on doing some investigating," he said. "Try not to be so obvious when you delve into this. Better still, hold off until I come back in town. I'll be back Friday and we can both help Danny with the case."

I clenched my jaw. Josh had never tried to curtail my investigating. "What do you mean about not being so obvious?"

"It's possible this man is involved in one or more of those murders. After seeing Remi's piece on TV and the three of y'all together, he suspected something was up."

"I suppose you're right," I admitted. "Remi and Tracy discussed her mother's murder on television last night and everyone in Allemand Parish knows my reputation for jumping in with both feet. I'll try to restrain myself." I paused a short moment. "By the way, I miss you."

"Good, because I miss you too…a lot."

We ended our call on that nice note. Over the last year, Josh and I had shared a number of adventures—experiences I never got to partake in with Jim mainly because of his official positions, first as a NOPD homicide detective and then his job as chief of police here in Cypress Lake. I'd grown quite fond of Josh, but I wasn't ready to take the next step of moving in together. Even though Josh made me feel wanted and needed and I enjoyed his company, Jim would always be the love of my life.

The twins got along well with Josh, but I felt sure they would object to having him move in with us. I'm afraid they would look upon such a situation as being disloyal to their father.

I heard Danny mumbling and Rachel asking him if he was in pain. I returned to the other room to see if she needed help.

"I could use something to eat." Danny's voice still sounded slightly groggy, but he had started to look more alert.

The fact he wanted to eat was a good sign. I saw relief in Rachel's face. She wasn't the only one.

While Rachel prepared a sandwich for Danny, Remi showed me the notes she and Rachel had been working on while I was on the phone.

"Remember Tracy said she had a genealogy book with her family tree and would make a return trip to Mobile to pick it up?"

"Sure."

"Rachel knew a lot of the names, so we started making a tree of our own starting from Charles Haydel. When Tracy comes back with the book, we can fill in the blanks."

"Sounds good. We might discover a long-lost relative who had been cut out of the family fortune and is intent on taking revenge."

I glanced at the list. I had only heard these names a day ago, but I was curious to learn more about them. *Curiosity killed the cat.* "Oh, my goodness. I forgot all about Katy. I need to check on her. She probably needs water and the litter box must be stinky." I made a fake grimace. "My favorite task."

"But she's one of your babies and you wouldn't trade her away for anything," Remi teased.

I wholeheartedly agreed. "She was my first child."

"Really? You had her before the twins were born." Remi seemed surprised. "Didn't she get jealous when you brought them home? I always heard that cats would jump into the crib and try to smother the baby."

Rachel and I both burst out laughing. "Remi, that's an old wives' tale," Rachel said, almost choking.

"No, she never has shown any jealousy," I said. "She and the twins get along great. I adopted her as a tiny kitten about two years before they were born. So, I guess that makes her a senior kitty now." I didn't like the idea of Katy's growing old.

Remi gave a faux pout. "I believed everything Grandma told me." Then she giggled. "Thanks for breaking my heart."

"Oh, get out of here," I said. "I'm going over to my house to take care of my fur baby. Be back in a few." It felt good to laugh at something silly.

I unlocked the door and stepped inside my house. As usual, Katy greeted me with her soft little meow. I scooped her up in my arms and petted her as I walked into the kitchen to check on her food and water bowls.

After taking care of the cat's needs, I played with her for a while so she wouldn't feel neglected. I was about to leave when my house phone rang. Hardly anyone calls on the landline except scam robocallers. I decided to answer anyway.

"Leave the murder cases alone," a live, not recorded, female voice said. "You'll be sorry if you don't."

"You've been watching too many crime dramas on TV." I disconnected immediately, hoping my voice hadn't revealed how threatened I felt. Normally I would've brushed off the call, but with someone shooting at Tracy and Danny, I took this one seriously.

The female caller surprised me. A menacing phone call would normally be done by a man. On second thought...I should know better. Women can be as dangerous as men. My late sister-in-law Anne, Steven's first wife, was murdered by a woman.

Were we dealing with a woman and not the man from the café? Or were these two collaborating in an attempt to stop the murder investigation?

I ran back next door. Believe me, my increased pulse rate wasn't simply from lack of exercise.

When I opened the door and entered the Marchands' kitchen, Remi met me with an expression that mirrored my own concerns. "What?"

"I received a phone call from an unknown female," she said. "She demanded I leave the investigation alone or I'd be sorry." Her usually calm voice sounded as shaky as I felt.

I blew out a long breath. "Me, too. Basically, she made the same threat to me."

"Danny's not happy about this new development. He doesn't even know about your call."

"I imagine he's not overjoyed," I said. "So, what's going to happen next?"

"We were waiting for you to come back before discussing anything."

"I'll bet this means you and I will be ordered to leave any investigating to the police."

"Probably. But I still have an obligation to report the news." Remi gave me a sidelong glance. "I could always use an assistant."

I followed Remi into the living room. Danny motioned for us to have a seat.

"Before we get started discussing anything," I said. "I need to tell you that I received a threatening phone call on my house phone. From what I gather, the call was similar to Remi's."

Danny groaned. "What did y'all do that would upset someone enough to start a campaign to stop the investigation and put all of you in danger?"

Remi raised her hands, palms up, in frustration. "My piece on the murders may have stirred up certain people, possibly causing Tracy and me to be in danger, but why Susan?"

"Because everybody in town knows I love to get involved in murder investigations," I said. "Whoever saw us at the Court House

Café believes we mean trouble for them. I have a strong feeling about the man who I saw there at the time. Now these phone calls were from a woman. Are these two involved together? Or is the man using a voice-changing device to throw us off?"

"I want you ladies not to go anywhere together," Danny said. "Is that clear?"

"You mean you want us to leave the investigating to law enforcement," I said.

"Don't go anywhere together or meet up again for lunch or such. Also, don't give the appearance you're doing any research, like going to the library or talking to anyone that could possibly be connected to Melanie's case or her mother's. And if you go out alone, be aware of your surroundings."

"Gramps," Remi said. "I have a job as an investigative reporter and this one is a story I need to look into. A woman I interviewed was shot at and a law enforcement officer hit. Even if that officer wasn't my grandfather who could have been killed, I would want to do the story."

"Are you still going to work on this case?" I asked Danny.

"You bet I am," he said in a steady voice. "Tomorrow I intend to cut down on the pain meds and I'm going to get back on it."

Rachel shook her head and released an audible sigh. "I knew you would do this. Listen to me, Danny Marchand. You are not going to do this by yourself. The three of us will help you in any way we can." She emphasized "any way."

I jumped into the conversation. "Josh will be back Friday. He already told me he wanted to help."

Danny didn't say anything for a long moment. He didn't look happy. "I'm sure Ronnie wouldn't agree with you civilians participating in this investigation. It's against department policy. At any rate, I'll be glad when Josh returns. Then I won't be so outnumbered by women."

I found it difficult to hide my smile.

~ * ~

"Making threatening phone calls was not what I'd had in mind when I told you and the others to lay low," he shouted into the phone. "This only keeps things stirred up."

"But we don't have time to lay low," said the woman on the other end of the line. "They could figure out at any time who we are and what we're up to."

"They don't know a thing. We hold all the cards."

"Not anymore. All those people whose scandals you held over their heads are dead now and we still don't have that ruby. We still don't have justice for the lives we had to live because of them."

"Trust me in this, Sis. Doing things like making threatening phone calls only makes them and law enforcement more determined. I made a mistake by asking your boy to get rid of the Lassiter woman. The sheriff's people want to find the person who shot their man. I'm warning you. Do not take matters into your own hands again."

Eleven

Wednesday, July 16

Spending the night in my own home took an act of congress. Rachel and Danny both objected on the grounds of my safety. Although I enjoyed their company, I needed time to myself to decide what my next move would be. Even when Remi offered to stay with me, I nixed the idea. She seemed offended, which I hadn't meant to do.

Remi and I are kindred spirits in that we both have to find the answers, no matter the consequences. I'll try to make it up to her later.

My intuition kept telling me that the man I saw at the café had had something to do with the attempted murder of Tracy and Danny. The woman who made those calls to me and Remi and me most likely had a connection to him. I needed to find out the man's identity. I wanted to jump in my car and drive to the Court House Café.

If I gave in to my intuition and left, Danny would immediately have deputies on my trail and take me into protective custody. I'm probably not exaggerating, considering last night.

I thought about the man for a few more minutes, and then made up my mind. I grabbed my purse and keys and left the house. All the way to downtown, I ran through the possible scenarios.

The man may have decided not to return after what had happened. Maybe he didn't believe I was smart enough to put two and two together and he would be seated in the café reading the newspaper and drinking coffee as if nothing had happened. Then there was always the chance he'd had nothing to do with any of this. That was one possibility I didn't believe likely. I'd be willing to bet my last dollar that one or the other of my first two ideas would be what I'd discover there.

I pulled into a vacant parking spot close to the entrance of the café and sat for a long time deciding whether to go inside. *What the heck? I'm here now.* This would be a wasted trip if I chickened out. I reached for the door handle and started to exit my car.

My heart thumped. There he stood in front of the café with a newspaper tucked under his arm. Staying put, I retrieved my phone from my purse and snapped two pictures, zooming in close to his face on my second shot.

He suddenly turned in my direction. I ducked out of sight, hoping he hadn't seen me. I don't know how long I hid from view, but when my back started cramping, I slowly raised up far enough to see over the dashboard.

The man had begun walking away from my location. I watched him for a while until he strode around the front of a blue car parked at the curb and entered the vehicle. I started my car and waited for him to pull out of his parking spot.

I followed him down the street, trying to be inconspicuous, but I suspected not very successfully. He kept looking in his rearview and side mirrors. I wanted to keep following him, but decided against it.

Better safe than sorry. I memorized his license plate number and turned off at the next street. I pulled over to the curb and rummaged through my purse for paper and pen to write down the number before I forgot it.

If Danny wasn't too mad at me for striking out on my own, he might agree to run the plate number to identify the car's owner.

I anticipated a less-than-warm reaction upon my return to the Marchands' home. Rachel greeted me with the look a disobedient child might receive from her mother. I almost expected to be grounded and sent to my room.

"I know. I know. I shouldn't have gone off by myself. But I have a possible clue as to the identification of the man at the café."

~ * ~

He could have sworn someone had been following him, but the car turned off onto another street. He must be getting paranoid. As the leader, so to speak, of the group, he had a big responsibility to keep the secret of their activities from becoming public. Every one of them, including him, could end up in prison or worse.

Before the news broke about the cold case reopening, his main goal had been to locate the ruby. Now his mission had taken on an added urgency...to keep the group from getting caught. They knew all the secrets of the Haydel dynasty. A lot of good that had done. The red gem would not only provide financial satisfaction and an escape from this place of secrets and lies, but also make up in some way for the humiliation they'd all suffered growing up.

Twelve

Thursday, July 17

I had managed to spend another night sleeping in my own bed instead of Rachel's guest room. The only bad thing about the time spent here was the loneliness I felt being the only one there. If Katy hadn't curled up next to me last night, I firmly believe I would have changed my mind about sleeping in my house and returned next door.

Before heading to Rachel's, I checked to make sure Katy's food and water bowls were filled and the stinky litter box scooped out. The things we do for our four-legged children.

After walking halfway across the yard, I spotted Tracy Lassiter as she turned into the Marchands' driveway. I waited for her to exit her car and walked over to her. She slung her purse over her shoulder and then retrieved a briefcase from the front seat.

"I located the family tree book and a few other items which could contain valuable clues about my mother's murder." She patted the briefcase to indicate its contents. "I don't how the sheriff's men didn't find all this during the original investigation."

I felt a tingling at the base of my neck. "What kind of items?"

"There were two journals. One belonged to my grandmother Anne LeBlanc and the other one was written by Harriet Haydel, my great-great grandmother, I think."

"The detectives probably didn't bother with those journals because they weren't written by your mother, whose murder they were trying to solve. Sometimes law enforcement has tunnel vision."

She frowned. "Or one-track minds."

I agreed. "Come on inside." I gave her a sidelong glance. "How are you since the shooting?"

Tracy's expression sobered. "Still a little shook, but I'm getting better. How is Danny? I'm sure he took a bullet meant for me."

"He grumbles constantly about not being able to use his arm yet like he used to. Other than that, he's fine."

We stepped inside the Marchands' kitchen and greeted Rachel and Remi, who I'm sure were on their third or fourth cup of coffee by then.

"Tracy, I didn't expect you back so soon," Remi said.

"I made record time coming back from Mobile. Good thing there weren't any police patrolling the interstate."

Remi eyed her with curiosity. "What's all the stuff you've got with you?"

"The family tree and two journals. The earliest one has entries written in the nineteen-twenties."

Rachel perked up. "That journal must belong to either Charles or Harriet Haydel."

"Harriet. The other one belongs to my grandmother, Anne LeBlanc." Tracy placed the book and envelope on the table. "I didn't get a chance to read but a few lines in either one. I grabbed these up and left in a hurry. All the way there and back, I felt as though someone were following me."

"What kind of vehicle?" I asked.

"There was a white pickup. The driver seemed to stay about two or three cars behind me. I know white pickups are not unusual in Louisiana, Mississippi, or Alabama."

"He followed you both ways?" Remi asked.

Tracy tilted her head slightly to one side. "As near as I could tell. The second vehicle could have been a different white truck."

Danny walked into the kitchen with his cell phone in his hand. He greeted Tracy. "I thought I heard your voice. You must have found some new information."

"I'm hopeful these journals will be helpful. I'll leave these with you to go over." She turned as if to leave.

"Stay, have a seat. Actually, I'm glad you ladies are all here," Danny said, pulling a chair out for Tracy. He seated himself on a barstool. "Ronnie is on his way over to speak to us about the case."

This didn't sound good to me. "I suppose this means the end of our inclusion in the investigation."

Danny rubbed his hand over his chin. "I'll simply let him say what he has to say. I don't like the idea of any of you getting involved, considering what's happened."

I was pretty sure then that our official investigating days were over.

"Tracy, you are the most vulnerable of the group," Danny continued. "It's obvious to me that whoever is behind the shooting and the threatening phone calls has a vendetta against your family."

She widened her eyes. "What threatening phone calls?"

"Remi and I both received intimidating phone calls ordering us to stay out of the investigation." I glanced at Danny. "Tracy believes someone in a white pickup followed her on the way to Mobile and back again."

Danny frowned. "Did the truck follow you here?"

"I don't believe they followed me into your subdivision. But I'm not positive."

The sound of a vehicle turning into the driveway drew everyone's attention in that direction. Danny stepped down from the barstool and walked over to the door. A few minutes later he ushered Ronnie inside.

The sheriff looked taken aback by all the women in the room, but then he smiled. "Danny, you didn't tell me our discussion involved so many beautiful ladies."

I returned his smile. "Flattery won't get you anywhere with us."

Danny gave a fake grimace. "See what I have to put up with?" He motioned for Ronnie to have a seat on the second barstool and returned to his perch on the other one. "Not only do I have to deal with my wife hovering over me now, but also my granddaughter and, you might as well say, my adopted daughter."

Meaning me. His words reminded me I hadn't called my parents like I said I would. It had been a while since I'd spoken to them.

Ronnie cleared his throat. "Danny has assured me he wants to continue working on Melanie LeBlanc's murder and any other case stemming from it that warrants looking into."

Tracy narrowed her eyes. "What other cases might there be?"

Ronnie exchanged a glance with Danny. "You explain the situation."

"I discovered an invoice stuck behind the files in a box of evidence I searched through the other day. An invoice from the body shop where Anne LeBlanc's car was towed after the hit-and-run accident. The mechanic stated that the brake lines on her vehicle had been deliberately cut."

Tracy gasped. "Her death wasn't an accident?"

"Looks like it," Danny said. "That's why I believe a person or persons have a vendetta against your family, and it has been going on for years." He turned to Ronnie. "In addition to the phone calls Remi and Susan received, Tracy believes someone followed her all the way to her home in Mobile and back."

Ronnie arched his eyebrows. "I agree with Danny about the vendetta, Tracy. I think we would be wise to put you in protective custody for a while, or at least have a deputy outside your place twenty-four seven."

She frowned. "Exactly what would protective custody entail?"

"Being placed in a safe house or at your own place with a deputy stationed inside with you," Ronnie said. "We have three female deputies on the force now who could serve as security."

"Unless having the deputies outside means I can't leave the house, I would prefer those rather than inside."

Ronnie lifted his hands, palms out. "You could leave the house, but we would not be able to protect you if you do."

I could imagine why Tracy didn't want to be confined in a safe house. It seems she, as well as Remi, are kindred spirits with me. Still, she appeared worried enough to ask about the deputies' providing security.

"What if Rachel, Remi, and I help Danny with some of the work? Josh will be back from Baton Rouge Friday and he is willing to do any legwork." I held my breath, waiting for an answer. Ronnie's stern expression didn't give me much hope of a positive one.

"As sheriff, I'm responsible for anything that might happen to any civilians if things go south, and I'm opposed to y'all being involved. I'd be going out on a limb if I agreed to allow y'all to do so."

My heart sank.

He paused a long moment. "But against my better judgment, that's exactly what I'm going to do," he continued. "Danny knows y'all better than I do. If he wants to allow any of you ladies and/or Broussard to play a part, I'll leave it up to him." He turned his gaze to me. "I know from past experience you're going to investigate on your own, no matter what either Danny or I say."

My reputation preceded me.

Thirteen

I watched Tracy catch up with Ronnie as he walked outside to his vehicle. She had a long, and what seemed like an intense conversation with him, before she left. I figured Ronnie's offer to put her up in a safe house or have deputies outside must have resonated with her in some way.

Hopefully, she would take him up on one of those options. Probably for the best. I didn't believe Danny thought it prudent for her to be involved to any extent anyway.

I couldn't recall a time when Ronnie had acted so serious and maybe even angry with me. His words rang true, all the same. Even if I had been forbidden to get involved, I would have most likely disobeyed the order when I thought I could find important information to help solve the mystery. I suppose Ronnie's attitude came from the fact that as sheriff he had more responsibility than in the past.

No one said a word for quite a while after Ronnie left. His offer to place Tracy in protective custody or at least have her under surveillance made everything seem a lot more dangerous.

Finally, Remi broke the silence. "Gramps, have we put you in a bad spot? I know the sheriff isn't happy about our involvement."

I agreed. "Especially with my reputation for getting into trouble."

"Ronnie's not happy because if anything goes wrong and one of you ladies or an innocent civilian gets hurt, he'll be the one who will ultimately get the blame." He eyed each one of us, including Rachel. "I am in a difficult spot. Although I'm retired as sheriff, I've been sworn in as a deputy for this case. In my mind, I'm taking on the responsibility for any civilians, including Josh, who are aiding me, even though as head of the department, Ronnie will get the blame if anything goes wrong.

"Right now, if I want to work these homicides, I have no other choice." He grimaced. "I can't remember a time when I selfishly put y'all in danger so I could work a case. Maybe it isn't such a good idea for y'all to be involved."

I realized then how much Danny wanted to solve these cold cases. I wanted to try to convince him we were volunteering for the investigation. "You're not selfish."

Rachel spoke up before I had a chance to elaborate. "Danny, we all know you don't want to put us in danger," she said. "Isn't there any possibility Ronnie could spare you a couple of deputies?"

"Not at this time, but maybe in a week or so," he replied. "So, if y'all want to help me with this case, or I should say cases, you must follow my directions to the letter," he continued. "We are dealing with dangerous people who don't want those murders to be solved."

"Gramps, you dealt with a lot of dangerous people when you were sheriff and before that as a detective," Remi argued. "I've been in a few iffy situations doing my job. Why is this any different?"

"Iffy is a lot different from dangerous. As sheriff, the teams I led were experienced officers who followed procedure and knew how to deal with criminals. Those officers can't be spared right now."

"And we're like a bunch of Nancy Drews," she said.

"But we're also people you love and care about and don't want anything bad to happen to," Rachel added.

He smiled at her. "Exactly."

I thought back to Monday, when I trespassed on private land and came close to having a serious eye problem courtesy of the graffiti artist. The comparison I made to myself with one of the too stupid to live protagonists came to mind. In the past, many of my actions were reckless. It seemed a miracle I still lived and breathed.

My children weren't in town at present, but now and when they returned, I'd have to force myself not to act on my curiosity and place myself in harm's way, for their sake. I am responsible for and dearly love Matthew and Caroline. I shuddered to think about the many times in the past when they could have been harmed by my reckless actions. I couldn't lose them or have them lose me.

Danny's voice broke into my thoughts. "Remi, what would you think about doing a short interview with me?"

"Gramps, I'd love to. Naturally, you would have full say over the content."

He came close to smiling. "Naturally. By the way, I sure hope you're not going to address me as Gramps in your interview."

His remark brought laughs all around and released some of the tension in the room.

Remi's lips spread into a wide grin. "I'll work up a rough draft of questions I would normally ask, and then you and I can work on the finishing touches."

"How about if I tell you what I want released first and then you make up the questions to ask me."

"That almost sounded like this would be more of a statement by you and not me interviewing you," she said.

"More or less." He proceeded to give her the information he wanted revealed. "You know the script. You've done it enough times."

"You're right, but I've never interviewed you."

Despite her usual professionalism, I thought Remi appeared nervous. Maybe she was worried about disappointing the grandfather she idolized.

"I'm not different from any other cop you've talked to in the past. Pretend you only met me a few minutes ago."

"I'll try," she said. "First, I need to contact my boss at the station and discuss doing this interview. If he okays it, then I'll get in touch with Jody, my photographer. I'll write up my script and we can go over it."

"Good deal," he said. "In the meantime, I've got a few calls I need to make and I want to look back over the crime scene photos for Melanie's murder."

"What can we do?" Rachel asked.

"I thought I heard Tracy say she'd brought some journals that belonged to her mother from Mobile. Were they Melanie's?"

"No, one belonged to her grandmother and the other was written by Harriet Haydel, Charles Haydel's wife. There's also a family genealogy record."

"Okay, you and Susan start going through those to see if you can come up with any new information."

"Oh, I almost forgot," I said. "I went to the Court House Café this morning and ended up following the man I had seen there before. I got his license number and a close-up of his face." I gave him a cautious look. "Can you trace the plate?"

"Send the picture and his plate number to my phone."

I could gauge his level of annoyance with me by the tone of his voice. Pretty high.

"When I get a few minutes," he added. He stepped down from the barstool and almost lost his balance.

Rachel automatically reached for him, but he brushed off her assistance.

"I'll be glad when I can get rid of this damn arm sling," he grumbled. "It's throwing my balance off." He strode toward his office.

Rachel shook her head in frustration. "Men. They simply can't admit they can't handle everything. Or even recognize they need to slow down a little bit."

"He sure is determined to solve these murders," I said. "He never would let any of us get involved otherwise."

"Danny's trying to prove he can still do the things he used to do years ago." She eyed me with concern. "Promise me you won't do anything foolish like going off on your own without talking things over with Danny and me."

"I promise." I really meant it, but I honestly didn't know if I could comply. In the back of my mind, I figured Danny didn't put much stock in my suspicions of the man at the café, so it might be a while before he got around to checking the license plate.

~ * ~

Tracy Lassiter surveyed the area outside the window of her newly rented townhouse. Cypress Lake had changed since she had moved to Mobile. There were new shops and new people in town. The Court House Café had even been remodeled since she lived there almost twenty years ago. The place used to be little more than a shack. Maybe Cypress Lake would be a nice place to live.

She shook off that thought. She knew why even as an adult she'd never returned to live in Cypress Lake. The memory of her mother's death haunted her. But there were so many blank spots in that memory. If only she hadn't been drinking, plus smoking pot. Maybe she could remember more details about her return home. Had she seen anyone leaving the house?

Her cell phone rang. She didn't recognize the number, but decided to answer anyway.

"Hello, sweetie," the male voice said.

"Dad?"

"Your one and only." His tone grated on her nerves.

"It's been a long time since you bothered to contact me. Why now?"

"Don't you think you made a big mistake by stirring up this mess with your mother's murder? You could be in big trouble."

"Why would I be in trouble? I went to the sheriff to find her killer."

He grunted. "You can't tell me you still don't remember killing her."

"I did not kill my mother," she shouted.

"You were stoned out of your mind when you phoned me. *'Daddy, I need help. I killed Mom.'*"

"If that's true, the sheriff would have arrested me. I found her dead."

"Don't come crying to me when they do arrest you. I won't help you a second time."

"Don't worry, Dad. I won't be needing your help." Tracy disconnected the call and threw her phone down. It landed on the coffee table with a thud.

Her heart beat so hard she thought it might jump out of her chest. *What should I do? I can't tell Danny about my father's phone call. He might reconsider me as a suspect. I didn't kill her. Or did I? Why can't I remember?*

Fourteen

Friday, July 18

I finally got around to phoning my father last night. We had a nice talk and I promised to keep in touch more often. It's not like my parents live way across the country. They're only an hour away in New Orleans. My problem is with my mother.

I spoke briefly with her because as soon as she came on the phone, she started in on me about how I had discredited my family name by *my* actions. Maybe she was correct in her assessment about my escapades. But she has always been on my case when she thought what I did lay beneath my social standing. Or should I say, *her* social standing. Mother left her West Bank blue collar roots behind when she married my father, as did her sister Rose, who married Dad's best friend.

Growing up, Mother always expected me to join in the activities of the snobby uptown New Orleans clique who belonged to our family's social set. These events, such as Mardi Gras balls, debutant cotillions, and other galas were her idea of how my life should be lived, although I did enjoy the Mardi Gras balls. Mainly because I love Mardi Gras.

Her dreams for me also included marriage to a young doctor or lawyer, not a homicide detective like Jim Foret. My brother Steven didn't fare much better with her when he decided to go into computer technology. The only difference was that he let her criticisms roll off him like water off a duck. Pardon the old cliché.

I have to admit that my conversation with Mother last night seemed different from her usual admonishments. I couldn't quite put my finger on why I thought so. Maybe she was mellowing.

The ring of my cell phone interrupted the rehashing of my former life. Josh's number appeared on the display. I smiled and answered the call.

"Hey," he said. "We're finishing up here, so I should be on the road in about an hour."

"Good, I'll be glad to see you."

"How's Danny?"

"Physically he's doing pretty good, although having his arm in a sling is frustrating for him," I said. "He's determined to handle this case without help from anyone."

"I thought he had you, Rachel, and Remi helping him."

I held my hands palms up. "We are, to a certain extent, but for all practical purposes we're simply doing paperwork."

"You mean he doesn't want you ladies getting into trouble."

"Exactly. Remi is giving the case some exposure. She and her photographer taped a short interview with Danny. It's supposed to air tonight on the six o'clock news."

Josh paused for a long moment. "Do you think he'll accept my help on the case?"

I had to laugh. "Yes, I'm sure he will. When Rachel, Remi, and I told him in no uncertain terms we were working on this case with him, he finally relented, but mumbled something to the effect that he would be glad when you returned because then he wouldn't be so outnumbered by females."

Josh laughed. "I'll bet y'all ganged up on him at his weakest moment, full of pain meds."

"Now, would we be so unkind?"

Still chuckling, he said. "Of course, y'all wouldn't."

Two hours later, Josh pulled into the driveway of my house. I greeted him with a hug and a big kiss, which he returned in kind.

At the same time, I fought with myself to erase the feeling of guilt about my relationship with him. The second anniversary of Jim's death was coming up soon. I had no idea how the memories would affect me on that day.

Later that afternoon, Josh and I walked next door in time to view Remi's interview with Danny on the news show. We settled in the Marchands' den to watch Remi do her stuff.

"I'm here with former Allemand Parish sheriff, Danny Marchand," she said. "Danny, I understand you have come out of retirement to head the investigation into the murder of Melanie LeBlanc, who died in two thousand one. What can you tell me about the reopening of this cold case? Why this particular case?"

"It's past time to give the family justice and some closure," Danny said. "Closure we weren't able to give them in the past. This is the only case left unsolved from my time as sheriff, so it's personal in a way. I'm reviewing all the evidence collected from the original murder scene and will be re-interviewing any witnesses from that investigation."

"I see you're still recovering from the wound you suffered during the shooting in front of city hall," Remi said, pointing to the sling on his arm.

"Yes, but I should have this thing off my arm in a few days." He lifted his arm briefly. "Although my doctor might have other ideas," he added.

"Were those shots aimed at Tracy Lassiter, Melanie LeBlanc's daughter? Do you have any suspects?"

He shook his head. "At this time, we can't say the shooter targeted Ms. Lassiter. As sheriff, I arrested a lot of bad guys. It's not like I don't have enemies. As to suspects, I can't comment on that at this time."

"Is there any other information you can give us today?"

"We have new information that indicates another death related to the LeBlanc family could be a homicide and not an accident as initially ruled. It's possible there is a connection to Melanie's murder. However, I'm not able to comment any further on that at this time."

~ * ~

His phone rang four times before he answered. He'd expected to be bombarded by frantic calls after Danny Marchand's interview.

"What are we going to do now?" she asked, a combination of fear and anger in her voice.

"There's nothing we can do at the moment. The police do not know who we are and what we are after."

"How can you be so certain?"

"There's no way they could know anything. Nothing has been said by the authorities about the ruby. If you recall, Tracy Lassiter told that reporter in her interview she had no idea what her great-great-grandfather did with the jewel."

"She could have lied. I'll bet it's in a safe deposit box somewhere. We'll never find the ruby."

"Stop talking so negatively. We'll simply have to be patient for a while longer."

"Our whole family has been patient for more than twenty years."

"You're right about that, but it's not like we can simply kidnap Tracy Lassiter and demand she give us the ruby." He gave an audible sigh. "I need to consider all the events and information learned since the sheriff reopened the case. I'll contact you when I have a plan in place."

He ended the call and sat quietly for a while. Coming up with a plan would not be easy. The new information about a related death mentioned by Marchand could only refer to the hit-and-run *accident* of Anne LeBlanc's. Her husband swore he had taken care of all the details. Obviously, he'd missed something. *Now he's no longer around to take the blame and I have no more leverage over him.* He thought a moment. *There is one man...*

Fifteen

About eight that evening, Josh left to check on his office and apartment, since he had come straight to my house from Baton Rouge. He said he would be back in about an hour or two. I decided to delve into Harriet Haydel's journal until he returned. Relaxing in my favorite chair, I started reading.

Her posts were interesting from a historical point of view, but otherwise boring until an entry dated July 17, 1929.

My beautiful girl Louise died yesterday as a result of a fall from a horse. Only five years old. Charles told me a snake frightened the mare, causing Louise to be thrown to the ground. I cannot bear the thought of viewing her in a coffin.

Ruth, her twin, is beside herself with grief. I should think she is too young to understand what happened, but apparently she is aware that Louise is not going to awaken from what appears to be sleep.

Charles is angry and upset, but blames the incident on his stable foreman and also the horse. No matter how many times I admonished him for allowing such young children to ride on those spirited beasts, he consented to their pleas to ride. The twins had him wrapped around their fingers from the very beginning of their lives. I believe he is feeling guilty at present because he allowed the girls so much freedom. He always blames someone else, which I know is a façade he uses when he cannot bring himself to admit he made a mistake.

To make matters worse, this morning an elderly Creole woman named Jennie arrived at our door with an ominous prediction. She stated to George, our butler, that Louise's death would be only the first of many to be inflicted on this family. He dismissed her firmly and ordered her off the property. I could tell by his demeanor after the incident he was shaken by her soothsaying.

As a matter of fact, I am also feeling unnerved. I nearly fainted when I heard about her prediction. For some unknown reason, the curse of the ruby ran through my mind, even though I know such beliefs are superstitions promoted by or encouraged by the devil. I must remove the notion from my mind. Charles would be furious if he knew I had even briefly considered the idea of a curse.

In the margin I saw a note written in the same handwriting but different colored ink. *"The first of many."*

I remembered Tracy made a comment about a number of other deaths in her family, which some people suggested may have been caused by the ruby's curse. At the time I thought she was referring only to her mother's murder, the death of her grandmother in the hit-and-run incident, and her great-great-grandfather Charles Haydel's fall from the balcony of his home. Could there be more information concerning the death of five-year-old Louise?

I continued reading, hoping to find more information about Louise's horseback accident. No such luck. The next few pages were interesting in a way by revealing Harriet's expression of grief and how she managed to return to a semi-normal life. Of course, the death of a child is one a parent never gets over. I hope I am never in such a situation. One interesting tidbit...the mention of the girls' two Burmese nannies.

After checking the time, I grabbed my cell phone and punched in Rachel's number. "Hope I didn't disturb you."

"Oh no," she said. "Danny is still engrossed in those files. Actually, I'd thought about phoning you, but didn't want to interrupt anything between you and Josh."

"He went to check on his office and apartment. Do you have news?"

"There's a couple of things I learned from the family genealogy book. Nothing to move our investigation along. I found it rather odd that each generation had only one child that survived to adulthood, all girls. Legitimate, that is."

"I'm willing to bet there's a lot of illegitimate children around. There's another man we don't have any info on. No one's even mentioned him. Did you find anything on Michael Richard, Anne's father?"

"Nothing earth shaking. As far as Michael Richard is concerned, his death was listed as February of nineteen fifty-nine. I found his death certificate in those other papers Tracy brought from her home. He died of liver disease. Cirrhosis."

"With all the social drinks those men seem to have imbibed, I'm not surprised."

"Oh, and Carl LeBlanc, Anne's husband, died of lung cancer," Rachel said. "Your turn. What do you have?"

"One question first," I said. "Remember the earlier mention about one death in Tracy's family being a relative who died in childbirth? Could that have been the death of a child not related to childbirth instead?"

"That's possible. Did you find something in Harriet's journal?"

I told her about five-year-old Louise being killed in a horseback riding accident and the prediction by the old Creole woman. "A notation in the margin read 'the first of many,' written in the same handwriting but different colored ink. Harriet also mentioned the two Burmese women who acted as nannies and how upset they were at the child's death."

"My goodness. This is getting interesting. I can understand why certain members of the family and even their servants might start to believe in the ruby's curse, especially the Burmese nannies." Rachel paused for a short moment. "Instead of going to bed, I think I'll check out the rest of those papers Tracy left here regarding the deaths of family members."

"If I find anything else of interest in the journal, I'll mark the page," I said. "We can get together in the morning."

I pondered how the story of the death of a child in a riding accident might have come down in family history as a death in childbirth. I suppose when family stories are repeated, generation after generation, the facts could become altered unintentionally. But in this case, it wouldn't surprise me if the facts were changed on purpose to cover up murders like the supposed hit-and-run death of Anne LeBlanc.

Sixteen

Saturday, July 19

The smell of freshly perked coffee greeted me as I lifted my head off the pillow. I glanced at the clock on my bedside table. The digital dial read 6:45. I smiled to myself. Josh and I had stayed up past midnight discussing my discovery in the journal. Well...not all of that time. I probably could have slept a few more hours.

"Time to rise and shine." Josh appeared at the door of the bedroom carrying a cup of coffee. His short-sleeved black t-shirt revealed his muscular arms.

My gaze fell to the mystery scar on his right arm above the wrist, which he refused to discuss. I pushed myself up and propped the pillows against the headboard. He handed the cup to me and sat on the side of the bed.

"Aren't you having one?"

"I had a cup already. Maybe I'll have another one later." He shrugged. "I've had my fill of coffee. It seems like all I had this past week."

"What do you mean? I'm sure you and all your friends had at least one nice dinner...like steak and baked potato with all the fixings."

"It seemed like I continuously had a cup of coffee in my hand," he said.

"Trying to stay awake during lectures?" I asked in jest.

"Almost. There were a few interesting new items to help with investigations, but on the whole, the material covered I already knew. The week away wasn't worth the cost of the seminar." He looked away for a short moment. "After you told me about your incident at the cemetery and then Danny getting shot, I was more than ready to come back home."

"I'm glad you're home now."

His expression grew serious. "Did you believe I was trying to put controls on your search when I told you to wait until I returned to investigate?"

"No, not really," I hedged.

"Come on now. Be honest."

"Okay," I admitted. "I did feel a bit controlled at the time. You had never done that. But after I thought about what you said, I realized you weren't trying to stop me from investigating, only advising me in order to keep me safe."

"You realized this before or after you followed the man from the café?" His brief smile made me wonder if he was teasing me.

"After." I gave a long sigh. "Delving into mysteries for me is like being addicted to a drug. But I need to restrain myself because of my responsibilities to my children."

"I have the same addiction about mysteries." He seemed preoccupied for a long moment.

I frowned. "Do you have something else on your mind?"

"No." He leaned toward me and kissed my cheek. "What's on your agenda for today?"

I eyed him for a few moments. His sudden change of subject seemed unconvincing. Could I be becoming paranoid? I decided to let my questions go for the time being.

Pushing the covers aside, I swung my feet over the side of the bed and sat facing him. "As to my agenda for today...remember I told you last night that I had written down the license number of the man from the café?"

He gave me a curious look. "Didn't you say you'd given the info to Danny?"

"I did, but I'm pretty sure he's not going to check on it. He doesn't believe that man has anything to do with the case or cases. Is there any way you can find out who the mystery man is?"

"I'll see what I can do."

"Those journals also await me," I said. "There might be more clues to the other murders or maybe what happened to the ruby."

"Sounds like a plan. You check the journals while I try to get through to motor vehicles." He rose from his spot on the bed and strode out of the room.

I decided to take a shower first, before getting started on Harriet Haydel's journal. Sometimes I think better with the warm water flowing over me.

After my shower I slipped into a pair of khaki shorts and a black t-shirt. The house was quiet—a little too quiet. I didn't even hear Josh on the phone.

"Josh?" No answer.

The sound of a vehicle pulling up in the driveway caught my attention. I looked out the kitchen window, surprised to see Josh exiting his truck carrying a large take-out bag from McDonald's. I had to laugh. From the size of the bag, he appeared to have bought enough food for an army. I opened the door to greet him.

"I have breakfast," he said.

"Looks like quite a spread."

He grinned. "Guess I got carried away. When I got over there and took in the smell of biscuits and bacon, I suddenly got hungry."

I filled two cups with coffee while he unpacked the food and set out our deluxe breakfast from McD's on the kitchen table.

Josh took a sip of his coffee. "I haven't checked for the license number yet. I got a call from an army buddy who recently got hired by Jennings PD. We talked for a while."

"As I recall, you told me your parents raised cattle outside of Jennings."

His eyes held a faraway look. "Yeah, we had a big piece of land. We had a pond and some wooded areas outside the pastures."

"Is your friend also from Jennings?"

"Yeah. We grew up together. He'll make a good cop." He began removing a bacon biscuit from its wrapper.

"Have you been back there to visit?"

"Not recently." He took a large bite of the biscuit.

I had the feeling he didn't want to answer more questions about his hometown and early life. His change of subject convinced me I was right.

"Did you say you were going to do more reading in one of those journals?"

"I do intend to read more." I told him about Rachel's opinion on the Haydel genealogy in relation to our investigation. He agreed with her conclusion.

After stuffing his food wrappers into the McD's bag, Josh rose from his seat. "I'll go check with motor vehicles now."

All families seemed to have secrets. Did Josh have a secret about his family? Were his parents even alive?

For certain there was one event he didn't want to talk about. How he'd gotten the injury to his arm. I assumed the wound had occurred years ago during one of his tours in Iraq. Maybe the whole event was too painful to talk about. A discussion for another time?

Seventeen

I looked up from my breakfast, surprised at the curious expression on Josh's face when he returned. "I ran the number you gave me. The system came up with an unexpected result. After all these years, I should know by now outcomes aren't always what we think they should be."

I frowned. "I hope I gave you the correct number. Who is the car owner?"

"The plate comes back to a Barbara Wilson, whose address is in Shreveport. The car is a 2018 blue Toyota. This info doesn't quite fit our scenario. I never expected the owner to be a woman."

"I see what you mean. I thought the registration would come back to a local man. But that sounds like the car. Shreveport is in the opposite end of the state. I wrote the number down from memory after I quit following the man and I wasn't exactly in the calmest state of mind." *What a letdown.* Then Josh gave me a little hope that my info might be correct.

"There are a number of possibilities. One, the man driving could have borrowed the car from Barbara, or...he stole it."

"Is a stolen car a possibility? Or did you throw that tidbit in to see if I caught it?"

An amused look crossed his face. "The latter. Not likely he's driving around in a stolen car. Although, there are people who would be bold enough to do that. The other possibility is he bought the car from her and has never changed the registration to his own name."

"That might be the most likely scenario. There are a lot of people who never get around to changing the name on the registration." I groaned. "But this sure threw a wrench into my expectations."

He shrugged. "That's the way these things go sometimes. We'll get a break sooner or later."

Josh's phone rang. He glanced at the number on the screen and answered. "Yeah, got back yesterday afternoon... Sure, I can come by there in about..." He glanced at his watch. "I can see you in about fifteen or twenty minutes." He ended the call. "Megan has some legwork for me to do for a case she's working on."

"This case must be a doozie for her to work on a weekend." I don't know why the idea of her working on Saturday surprised me. My sister-in-law was very devoted to her defense clients. She usually got the charges dropped or else worked a plea deal for them. It's a good thing she didn't represent any of those men who were charged with Jim's murder. They might have gotten off with a slap on the wrist.

Josh planted a kiss on my lips and turned to leave. "I'm not sure when I'll be back. Call you later."

Something had seemed off with Josh since he returned from Baton Rouge. Something I couldn't put my finger on. Could he be tired of me? Or did he want more from me than I could give him? Brushing off all those questions, I decided to do a Scarlett O'Hara and think about it all tomorrow. I had work to do right now.

I pushed my chair back from the table and cleared off the remains of the take-out. After disposing of those in the garbage, I returned to the bedroom in search of my laptop. My new focus became finding Barbara Wilson, although I didn't have much confidence in locating her. Barbara Wilson was a pretty common name.

She might have a Facebook page or maybe even a website. Couldn't hurt to check. I keyed her name into a search engine and hoped for the best. There were ten Barbara Wilsons listed. I started checking the first one. This one lived in New York. No Shreveport address on the second or third name.

By the time I got to number seven with no luck I felt extremely down, but I didn't want to give up. Three more to go. Here goes Barbara number eight. And nine...and ten. No luck.

My cell phone rang. I recognized the number as Rachel's and answered. "Hey, what's up?"

"I may have a clue about the identity of your man from the café," she said.

"How did you manage that?" My heartbeat quickened.

"It's kind of tentative, but I started looking at the photo you took of him outside the Court House Café. I remembered seeing him somewhere in town a while back. After searching my aging brain, I realized where. Carter's Bakery. I saw him talking to the woman behind the counter and overheard him call her Sis."

"Do you know what her name is?"

"Her nametag read Barbara."

"I can't believe this!" I screamed.

"What?"

"Sorry, I got a little excited."

"I'll say. Don't keep me in suspense."

"Josh ran the car's plate number and it came back to a Barbara Wilson. But she'd listed her address on the registration as Shreveport. That's got to be her!"

"That's quite the coincidence," Rachel said. "But I still don't understand why you believe this man has a connection to Melanie's murder."

"I don't have evidence to show he's connected. Just a strong feeling. I'm going to go over to the bakery now. Do you want to come with me?"

"I don't think it's a good idea for you and me to race over to the bakery together," Rachel said. "Everyone in town knows we sometimes collaborate on investigating. What if Barbara *is* involved in some scheme related to Melanie's death?"

"Then I'll go by myself. I suppose if we show up over there, Barbara could get suspicious. Although it's been a few days since you were there. She may not remember. Besides, I would love to have some crème-filled donuts. How about you?"

"Oh no, I'd never turn down one of those." Her tone sobered. "Try not to get your hopes up too high. Barbara is a common name. Please be careful."

"I will be careful. I promise. Talk to you later." Taking a deep breath, I grabbed my purse and tossed my phone inside. I knew Rachel was trying to tamp down my enthusiasm to keep me from being disappointed if "Bakery Barbara" tuned out to be Barbara Smith. In my mind this seemed too much of a coincidence for her not to be *the* Barbara Wilson.

Eighteen

The drive to Carter's Bakery only took ten minutes. A bell on the door announced my presence and the aroma of sugary treats greeted me when I entered the store.

I hadn't thought out what I would say or do when I came face to face with Barbara. Heck, it wasn't like she would immediately point a gun at me and tell me to get lost. Play it by ear and see what, if anything, I can discover.

A dark-haired woman emerged from a door behind the counter. Not Barbara. What a disappointment. In fact, I knew her from my volunteer work at our parish food pantry. She recognized me and smiled. This could be an advantage.

"Teresa, how are you?"

"As good as ever," she said. "Thanks to volunteers like you, I was able to get this job."

My face reddened. I hadn't been to the food pantry in quite some time. "How long have you been working here?"

She looked thoughtful. "Three weeks now."

"Are you working by yourself today?"

"Only until two, then Jenny Babin comes in to relieve me. Thank goodness I don't have to close tonight."

"Yeah, counting all the money is nerve-racking, especially on a Saturday. Isn't there another woman who works here? I know Jenny and you, but I didn't recognize the woman who waited on me the last time I came in here."

Teresa made a face. "You must mean the witch spelled with a B. Barbara Wilson. She quit yesterday. Said she might be going back to North Louisiana." She quickly changed the subject, as if realizing she had stepped over the line with her comment. "What can I get for you today, Susan?"

"How about a half dozen crème-filled and another four regular glazed donuts?"

"Coming up." She grabbed a box and began placing my order inside. "You must be giving a party or else you're having a serious sweet tooth day."

"Unfortunately, I had a longing for crème-filled donuts." I measured my words carefully. "I get the impression Barbara wasn't exactly your favorite person."

Teresa jerked her head up. "I'm sorry for the bad language. You're not going to report me to Mrs. Carter, are you? She doesn't like curse words at all. We can't even say *Oh my God* or *for God's sake.*"

"Wow, she is conservative. I wouldn't dream of reporting you. But why the bad feelings about Barbara?"

"Oh, one day she would say she knew how to run this place better than anyone else or she acted holier than thou. Then the next day she would be a victim. 'People looked down on me all my life,' she would say.

"Jenny got into it with her one day concerning a complaint Barbara had made about one of our bakers," she continued. "You know Jenny is the manager now. She's worked here for a couple of years, so she's the boss when Mrs. Carter isn't in the shop. Jenny set her straight."

"Sounds like Barbara was a mixed-up individual."

"You got that right. Her brother George came in here a lot to talk to her. He looked like a creep."

My heart thumped. *George? Could his last name also be Wilson?* "What caused you to think that?"

She gave a brief shrug. "I don't know. I had a bad feeling about him. Haven't you ever gotten that kind of vibe about someone you've met?"

"Yes, I have. Quite a few times."

~ * ~

On the drive back to Cypress Lake, Josh put the truck on cruise control. His mind seemed to be there as well. He had probably made something out of nothing about what happened in Baton Rouge. He'd never felt insecure about a relationship or a choice, but his apprehension in this case had almost gotten the best of him. *I'm competing with a ghost.*

He parked his truck in the small lot on the side of Megan's law office and went inside. Handing a folder across the desk to her, he said, blandly, "I hope this is everything you need."

"Something is troubling you. I can tell by your voice," she said. "Are you and Susan okay? I didn't mean to interrupt your return home."

He silently cringed. If anyone could chip away at a situation and get answers, she would be the one. "No, we're fine."

Megan eyed him with suspicion. "Come on. You and I have known each other for a long time. What's going on? Talk to me." She motioned for him to take a seat in the chair next to her desk.

Josh briefly rubbed his hand over his chin. Against his better judgment, he sat. "I met a guy at the seminar named Dave Falcon who used to work for NOPD. He couldn't say enough good things about Jim Foret. Maybe he didn't intend to, but he made me feel like I would never measure up to the man. I might be paranoid, but I got the impression he was feeling me out about my intentions with Susan."

She looked doubtful. "Do you believe he has designs on her?"

He shook his head. "As far as I know, Susan hasn't had any contact with Falcon since Jim's death. Susan had a deep love for Jim. For all I know, she still loves him."

"Look, Jim *was* a wonderful man. Susan will always love him and feel a strong connection to him. He's the father of her children. You and she share a different relationship. That doesn't mean she can't feel love for you.

"Dave Falcon and another detective named Phil Berthelot worked with Jim for years," she continued. "The three of them were close friends. So maybe he's being protective. Have you told Susan about meeting Falcon?"

"With the anniversary of Jim's death coming up in a few days, I didn't want to bring it up. I didn't know how she would react."

Megan narrowed her eyes. "I've never known you to be less than straightforward about anything. How has Susan been acting about the upcoming date?"

Hell, I must've sounded like either an insecure school boy or an inconsiderate bastard. He cleared his throat. "Since I've been gone for a week, I'm not sure about what's she's feeling inside, but I have my suspicions. Prior to my trip, I'd catch her staring off into space. One day we were all playing a board game and Caroline said something like 'my daddy used to play this with us.' Matthew gave me a cold stare. She changed the subject quickly."

"Susan is in an awkward place, especially with Matthew." Megan gave a long sigh. "I sure hope he's not going to start acting up again. Anyway, how do you think Susan is faring since you returned?"

"My opinion is she's using this cold case revival to keep her from thinking about his death. She's probably going to mark the date somehow, even though the kids won't be here. I can't believe she would let the day go by without having some kind of service or at least put flowers on his tomb."

Megan's steady gaze met his. "I'll be straight to the point."

Josh raised his eyebrows. "Aren't you always?"

Her brief laugh didn't contain humor. "I am that. Steven tells me so all the time. First of all. You should definitely tell Susan about meeting Dave Falcon. If by some strange coincidence she discovers you met him in Baton Rouge and didn't mention it, she will be upset with you. It could become a trust issue."

"You're right," he agreed reluctantly.

Megan pointed her index finger in his direction. "Now, a straightforward question. Although I already know the answer. What *are* your intentions with Susan?"

"I love her. I want to marry her."

Nineteen

I wanted to rush over and tell Rachel about George, Barbara Wilson's brother. Harriet Haydel had other ideas.

For unknown reasons, her journal called to me from my chair where I'd left it last night. After the account of her daughter's death, there weren't any entries of interest. Could my subconscious be trying to tell me more attention-grabbing items came later?

I took one of the donuts in a napkin along with a cup of coffee and settled into my security blanket chair. The wingback curved around me, keeping me, in my crazy mind, safe from the world.

The crème-filled donut tasted fabulous. I needed to keep only a few at my house and leave the remainder with Rachel or I would be going into sugar shock. I wiped the sticky stuff from my hands with some wet wipes, and then took a few sips of coffee. Time to dig into Harriet's journal.

The first entry I turned to definitely caught my attention. Another death recorded by Harriet.

August 15, 1929
Considering how beautiful this day started out, it ended horribly with the death of Mya, one of our Burmese nannies, during childbirth.

I became aware of her pregnancy early on and I knew with great certainty the stable foreman could not be the father as she and her sister Chun claimed. Charles more or less admitted to me the child was his.

The infant, a boy, survived the birth. God forgive me. I couldn't bear to look at him and turned his care over to Chun. She agreed to locate a wet nurse for him, and otherwise she would raise him.

August 18, 1929

We buried Mya at the rear of the family cemetery. I commissioned a small headstone to mark her grave. Otherwise, there would be no recognition of her service to me and the girls. She would have been dumped unceremoniously into the ground. I watch Chun frequently from my window. Sadly, she visits her sister's grave every day and cries for quite a while during her visits. Poor girl, alone in a strange country without her only family. My time in Louisiana has led me to forget my Christian upbringing. I find the act of forgiving Charles for his adultery impossible. When I remember my sweet daughter's death only a month ago, I am angry with Charles and I am angry with God.

Wow, the death from childbirth really happened. My heart thumped faster. My discovery may mean nothing, but I had the feeling the event could be the next step in the quest to find answers about the numerous family deaths.

Even though the deceased didn't qualify as a family member in the true sense of the word, the child did have the bloodline of Haydel. Looked like my theory about Charles Haydel being the only man who had remained faithful to his wife didn't hold water.

I had a hand on my cell phone, ready to dial Rachel, but the sound of a vehicle pulling into my driveway stopped me. A few minutes later, Josh opened the kitchen door and stepped inside.

"Hey," I said. "I didn't expect you back until later."

"Megan's job involved a short trip to Kenner to pick up some paperwork from her client. Piece o' cake." He tilted his head to one side, eyeing me with curiosity. "You look pumped about something."

"You could say so. Come check this out."

He walked over and leaned closer to view the journal. I pointed out my discovery on the page and explained the event.

He sat across from me on the sofa. "Nothing should surprise me anymore, but there are times when unexpected information pops up it does. You know what they say about secrets lying behind closed doors and the other old cliché about skeletons in the closet."

"We could discover more skeletons hidden in the Haydel family closets before this investigation is over." A thought occurred to me. "Oh, I found more information about Barbara Wilson."

He perked up. "No kidding. Who is she?"

I told him about Rachel's recognition of the man after having seen him in Carter's Bakery, and filled him in on the opinions of Barbara by her co-workers. "She has a brother named George. I'm pretty sure he's the man from the café.

"I'm not certain why I believe she and the man from the café fit into this scheme," I continued, "but I have a strong feeling they do."

"You could be right," he said. "Your instincts have been spot-on in the past."

"Is it possible to locate a photo of Barbara Wilson? I mean, like a driver's license picture?"

"I can try to get one, but why do you want a picture?"

"I'm curious to see what she looks like and if she bears any resemblance to the guy at the cemetery who tried to spray me with paint."

Twenty

Josh shifted in his seat. "Uh...I met someone in Baton Rouge who knows you."

"Who?" I couldn't imagine who this person could be.

"A guy who used to work for NOPD. Dave Falcon. You know him?"

I smiled. "I do. He and another detective, Phil Berthelot, worked with Jim for many years." I eyed him with curiosity. "Dave Falcon at a PI seminar? Odd, unless he's not with NOPD any longer."

"He's not. After Berthelot retired, Falcon decided to get out and start his own investigation firm." He made a face. "Nice guy, but more competition for me in this business."

"Is his office in New Orleans?"

"Yeah, it is."

"With all the crime Cypress Lake has had in the past few years, I can't see where Dave would be any kind of threat to your business."

"You're right about the crime in this town, but a lot of the problems here carry over into NOLA." He tilted his head slightly to one side. "So, you haven't had any contact lately with any of Jim's old comrades from NOPD?"

What an odd question. "No, not since the memorial I arranged."

"Falcon knows you and I are together. He didn't come right out and ask me about my intentions, but he sure hinted about it."

"That sounds like we're seeing each other in secret. It's not like we kept our relationship hidden, but we didn't announce the details to the world. Even if he somehow knew about us, why would he be questioning you about your intentions with me?"

"Your guess is as good as mine. He certainly praised Jim a lot." He averted his eyes for a short moment. "Sorry, that didn't come out like I intended."

I saw the light about Josh's strange behavior and I didn't like it. This conversation seemed to be headed where I didn't want to go. "Why didn't you tell me earlier about meeting Dave?"

"Because the anniversary of Jim's death is coming up next week and I didn't want to bring up the bad memories."

I stared at him for a minute or so. "Telling me about meeting an old associate of Jim's would not have brought up bad memories. There's something else going on. I've noticed a difference in your demeanor ever since you returned from Baton Rouge."

He didn't answer right away. "After hearing praise after praise about Jim Foret's attributes from Falcon, I started wondering whether I could ever measure up to him with you. Matthew will forever compare me to his father. I've seen the looks he gives me."

I had never seen this Josh before. His insecurity appeared to come out of nowhere.

"I'm having a hard time understanding why praise for Jim from a fellow police officer would make you feel unworthy. You're not Jim. You have a different personality. Jim is dead.

"Matthew may never accept anyone else in my life," I continued. "Whoever I have a relationship with is my choice. He's a child."

Tears brimmed in my eyes. My throat tightened, but I forced the words out of my mouth. "I can't have this conversation right now. If you didn't intend to stir up my memories of Jim, your plan didn't work. Please leave. I'd like to be alone for a while."

Without speaking, he stood and left the house.

The moment I heard his truck drive away, I regretted my words. For weeks I'd told myself I would not fall apart on this anniversary of

Jim's death. Two years had passed since that awful day. I guess I'm not as strong as I've pretended to be. Or maybe I'm still not ready for a new relationship.

Grabbing my purse, I went outside to the car. No, I didn't intend to chase after Josh. I needed to talk to Jim.

The drive to the cemetery took about fifteen minutes. I drove through the gates and down the gravel road to the mausoleum. Sitting in the car for a few minutes, I stared at the white marble structure that lay behind rows of gravesites marked by crosses and above-ground tombs.

Taking a deep breath, I exited the car and walked toward the front wall of the mausoleum. Images of Jim's coffin slipping from view inside the narrow slot flooded my mind. My legs felt weak. I managed to make my way to the concrete bench and plopped down on the hard surface.

I took five yoga-style deep breaths and whispered, *Jim, I know you can't answer me directly. Although I'd give anything to hear your voice. I don't know what to do about Matthew's behavior problems or my feelings for Josh. Matthew feels anger toward me. He thinks I'm betraying you. Sometimes I feel like I am. Please help me figure this out.*

"Susan?"

I jerked my head around, heart thumping. "Tracy, what are you doing here?"

Her expression seemed tight and strained. "I didn't mean to scare you. I need someone to talk to about the night of my mother's murder."

"I'm not sure I'm the one to speak to about that. Is there something you've remembered about that night?"

She shook her head. "Something I *can't* remember."

My interest was immediately piqued. "Come sit down." I patted the space next to me on the bench. "How on earth did you find me here?"

She began wringing her hands. "On my way to speak to Danny about the problem, I chickened out. Then I saw you leaving and decided to follow and talk to you. I hope I can trust you."

"Trust me with what? If you know something that will help to find your mother's killer, you need to speak to Danny."

Her eyes teared. "I...I don't know for sure...The killer might be me."

Before I could react to her statement, a hard object poked me in my back. Tracy let out a squeal. I realized the object could be the barrel of a gun.

"Shut up, Ms. Lassiter, or I'll shoot your friend," a man said.

A second man grabbed Tracy by her arm and forced her off the bench. He held a gun to her head. "Come with us now or both of you will be dead."

The man who held Tracy wore a bandana covering his face from nose to below the chin. I attempted to get a look at the man behind me. Big mistake.

His gun came toward me in slow motion. A muffled pop. A sharp pain pierced my shoulder. I tumbled off the bench and onto the ground. A vague sense of Tracy being escorted roughly away by the two men faded into darkness.

Twenty-one

Sunday, July 20

I heard whispered voices mentioning my name. In my altered state I wondered if I had died. No, I couldn't be dead. My kids...what would they do without me? A faint odor, like disinfectant, wafted over me. Hospital...I'm in the hospital. Not dead. I tried to open my eyes, but my eyelids felt like they had weights taped to them.

"Hey, I think she's coming to." I recognized my brother Steven's voice. "Susie, can you hear me?"

I finally managed to open my eyes partway and mumbled an acknowledgement.

Rachel came closer to the bed. "Thank God. We were so worried."

"What day is this?"

"Sunday," she said. "Yesterday evening you had surgery to remove the bullet from your shoulder."

The fog in my brain suddenly disappeared. "Yesterday? Oh no. Where's Danny? I've got to tell him about Tracy."

"What about Tracy?" Steven asked. "Did she shoot you?"

"No, no. A man shot me." I tried to push myself up. A terrific pain shot through my arm.

Rachel clasped my hand. "Calm down. Steven, go tell Danny to get in here." She brushed her hand gently up and down my arm. "Try not to get upset. You'll mess up your stitches."

Before Steven could leave, the door to my room opened. I recognized Doctor Theriot as he walked in, followed by a nurse. "I'm glad to see you're awake, but not if having company is getting you all riled up." He indicated my visitors with a glance in their direction. "I'll let you know when she can have visitors again."

Steven and Rachel left the room, both glancing back with worried looks.

"Please, I need...to speak to Danny. It's urgent. Tracy might be dead by now." I attempted to get out of the bed, but got tangled up in the bedcovers and all the tubes. A twinge in my arm reminded me of my connection to an IV needle.

The nurse grabbed my arm and not so gently held me in place.

"Whoa, hold on," Doctor Theriot said. "Before I let anyone else in the room, you've got to calm down. Take a deep breath."

My throat tightened. I tried not to cry, but the tears started flowing, followed by heavy sobs.

He turned to the nurse and ordered medication in a mix of medical jargon and plain English. She left the room.

They intended to relax me all right. Not going to happen. Not until I filled Danny in about what had occurred at the cemetery.

"Please let...me...speak to Danny before you...knock me out."

He looked at me for a long moment. "Against my better judgment, I'll allow you to speak to him."

He opened the door and called Danny's name. "She says it's urgent. I assume this has to do with whoever shot her."

I heard Danny's muffled voice and another male voice. The second man seemed to be asking to come in also.

"No, only Danny," a clearly frustrated doctor stated. "I'm coming in with you. The moment she starts getting upset, you'll have to leave."

Danny strode into the room, his expression somber. Doctor Theriot followed him, but leaned against the wall, remaining in the background.

"Do you know who shot you?" Danny's voice sounded soft, but at the same time direct.

"I don't know names, but there were two men, both wearing bandana masks. One held a gun to my back and the other grabbed Tracy. I tried to see the man who held the gun on me, but that's when he shot me. The last thing I remember was those two men forcing Tracy away."

"Were you and Tracy meeting up for some reason?"

"If you mean a planned meeting, the answer is no." I took a deep breath and squeezed my eyes shut.

Danny took hold of my hand. "Everything's going to be okay."

"I hope Tracy can be found and that she's all right."

"I'll do my best to find her. How did she know your location?"

"She told me she'd planned to speak to you about something that happened the night of her mother's murder, but she chickened out. She saw me leaving the house and followed me. I guess those guys were following her."

He frowned. "Did she say why she decided not to tell me?"

"She did sort of. I asked if this could be an incident that she'd suddenly remembered happening the night of the murder. But she said *'something I can't remember'* quote, unquote. She wanted to know if she could trust me. What she said next threw me for a loop. She said the killer might be her."

"You mean Tracy herself?" Danny's jaw muscle twitched. "What happened after that?"

"The two men came up behind us and you know the rest."

"Can you give me any kind of physical description of these men? Did you see a car?"

"The man who grabbed Tracy appeared to be maybe twenty or so. From what I could see of his skin color, he looked white, but with an olive complexion. As for the other man, I couldn't tell you much about him. Everything happened so fast. I only saw the gun he had in his hand."

"Any car?"

Doctor Theriot interrupted our interview when the door opened. The nurse entered carrying a small tray with a syringe. I knew I would be out of it again for a while.

Danny turned to leave as the nurse started injecting the medication into my IV. I called to him. "Is Josh out there?"

"Not right now. He stayed up here all night. I talked him into leaving for a while. Do you want to see him?"

"Not yet." My words slurred as I started feeling the effects of the drug.

Danny nodded. "Let me know when you're ready to see him."

Would I ever be ready?

Twenty-two

Steven and Rachel more or less ambushed Danny as he stepped out into the hospital corridor.

"Has she calmed down?" Steven's voice cracked. "What's the deal about Tracy?"

"Did she tell you who shot her?" Rachel asked.

Danny held up his hands. "I can't tell you anything about what she told me. At least not yet. She didn't know any names. Tracy has been kidnapped by two men."

An uneasy expression crossed Steven's face. "Can we go back in?"

"I don't know. The nurse gave her something to relax her, so she's probably asleep by now. Doc Theriot is still in there with her."

"When he comes out, I'll ask if we can go back into the room." Rachel placed her arm around Steven's shoulder. "Don't worry. She's in good hands."

Danny glanced around the hallway. "Where'd Ronnie go?"

"He stepped out to take a call from the station," Rachel said. "He should be back shortly. Oh, there he is."

Ronnie Hart strode toward them and motioned with his hand for Danny to join him.

Danny stepped away from Rachel and Steven. "What's up?"

"My men discovered Tracy Lassiter's car abandoned a few streets over from the cemetery. I ordered a tow to bring the car to the garage."

"We need to find some security cameras in the vicinity of the cemetery," Danny said. "Susan couldn't give me too much in the way of description of the shooter or his partner. She said they kidnapped Tracy."

Ronnie squinted his eyes as if in thought. "I'm pretty sure there's a camera right outside the cemetery office by the main entrance gate and one close to the rear gate. I hope at least one camera caught what we need on tape."

"I'll get in touch with Ray Atkinson, the caretaker, to see if we can view the tapes." Danny pulled his cell phone from his pocket and made the call. Atkinson agreed to meet him at the cemetery.

Ronnie started walking down the hall. "Let's go check it out."

"Right after you."

Danny followed him out of the hospital and left with Ronnie in the marked sheriff's car.

Ray Atkinson greeted them in a small office inside the building near the entrance gate. His expression was clouded. "I hate to tell you this. The camera at the back gate would most likely have caught the whole scene. The damn thing has been malfunctioning for a couple of days. I hadn't gotten around to looking into having it fixed. I doubt there's any usable video on it."

Danny couldn't contain his disappointment. "Crap. What's the problem with the camera?"

"Don't know. It keeps cutting out. Sometimes we'd get video and other times nothing."

"How about the front camera? Maybe we can get lucky there."

Atkinson waved his hand. "Follow me." He led them to an even smaller room than the first, where an array of video equipment took up more space.

Danny exchanged a glance with Ronnie. "Kind of a tight squeeze in here."

The sheriff's large frame added to his own bulk didn't leave much room to move around or even breathe. Atkinson, on the other hand, with his short and skinny body, appeared quite comfortable with the space.

"Tell you what," Ronnie said. "I'll go take a look at the location of Tracy's vehicle. You stay and see if there's anything worth our while on the tape. I'll come back and pick you up in a bit."

Danny agreed. "Go ahead, Ray, start the machine. All this happened around noon yesterday."

Minutes went by and no vehicles passed through the gate. At five minutes past twelve, Danny recognized Susan's SUV turning into the driveway. He watched until her car disappeared out of the camera's view.

Shortly afterwards, another vehicle drove through the gate. He identified the car as belonging to Tracy Lassiter. Like Susan's car, Tracy's slipped out of camera range in a few seconds. Not far behind her, a white F150 double cab pickup drove much slower, possibly in an effort to conceal the fact that the driver had followed Tracy.

Danny rubbed his chin with his hand and thought back to a conversation with Tracy. She had reported being followed by a white pickup on the trip to Mobile and back. Although white pickups were a dime a dozen around here, he didn't believe in coincidence.

I'd be willing to bet my last dollar this is the same truck.

"Ray, cue the tape up to about thirty minutes later. Let's see if we can catch this truck leaving."

Forty minutes after it arrived, the white pickup showed up on the video, traveling toward the gate at a higher speed than when it had entered the cemetery. Not fast enough to attract attention, but definitely faster. Tracy's vehicle followed close behind.

Danny noted that the pickup turned right onto the street. Tracy's car went right as well.

"Can you make me a copy of this tape?"

"Sure thing," Atkinson said.

"I need to take a look at video from the back camera on the odd chance we got at least a partial view."

Atkinson moved to another screen and cued up the video from the back camera. The video flashed and crackled for a second or two. A shot of the mausoleum came into view.

Susan sat on a concrete bench, her back to the camera. Shortly thereafter, Tracy appeared and the two women began to have a conversation. Tracy sat next to Susan on the bench.

Danny's heart thumped. Two figures appeared behind them. The tape went to black. "Damn it. Keep playing the tape. I'm hoping the camera caught some action a little later."

The break in the video continued and then it suddenly picked up again. Susan lay on the ground and two men could be seen escorting Tracy away at gunpoint. At that moment, the video cut out again.

"I need a copy of that one also, including the breaks. That'll give me a timeline."

Atkinson agreed and slipped a CD into the machine.

"While you're making the copies, I'm going to take a walk back to the crime scene," Danny said. "By the way, why didn't you get the camera looked at?"

Ray shrugged. "Nobody expects the police to need video from a cemetery. Everybody in here has been dead and buried for a long time. The only reason we have a camera back there is to make sure none of our equipment gets stolen. Besides," he growled, "damn cameras cost a fortune. The city doesn't give me enough money for extras."

Danny raised his eyebrows and walked out of the claustrophobic room. Outside he inhaled a deep breath of fresh air.

Twenty-three

I vaguely remember Doctor Theriot and the nurse leaving the room. My eyelids felt heavy and I drifted off to sleep.

Jim came toward me, smiling. "You're going to be okay." Words similar to this he'd said before in another dream. I didn't understand the meaning at the time and still don't.

"How can I be? Everything has gone crazy again."

"You're going to be okay without me," Jim answered.

In the background to Jim's left, Josh appeared, an anxious look clouding his face. He moved closer.

Jim disappeared.

The next time I opened my eyes, I didn't see or hear anyone. For a few moments I thought everyone had deserted me. Then I saw Rachel curled up in a chair, dozing.

As if sensing I was awake, she sat up and gave me a relieved smile. "About time you woke up. You've been out for a while."

"How long is a while?" I returned her smile with a faint one of my own. "What time is it?"

She glanced at her watch. "Five-thirty p.m. Time for supper. The aide should be bringing your tray in any time now."

I made a face. The thought of food didn't appeal to me. "Is it still Sunday?" It seemed like days had passed since my shooting and Tracy's kidnapping.

"Yes, it is. I'm teasing about your long nap. You've only been asleep for about four hours." She gently patted my hand. "Can I get you something?"

"Information."

Rachel gave a frustrated sigh. "I don't have much to offer and I'm not going to let you get all riled up again. Danny left with Ronnie to go to the cemetery. I think they might be on a search for security video. That's all I know."

My heart sank. "But no word on Tracy?"

"Not that I know of. I'll see if I can find out anything. Doctor Theriot gave strict orders. Only one visitor at a time. If Steven is still out there, I'll send him in." She left the room.

I reluctantly agreed. I didn't have much hope about news of a rescue for Tracy or if she had made it out alive...*no, don't go there. She can't be dead. They're holding her hostage to get the ruby or maybe for any number of reasons.* I found the idea of Tracy having killed her mother unbelievable.

Instead of Steven, my attorney sister-in-law Megan peered inside the partially open door. "Steven left for a while. Since you have a restricted number of visitors, I decided to take his place."

"Come on in," I said.

Although Megan wore her shoulder-length blond hair in a casual style, she looked as if she'd stepped out of the beauty salon a few minutes ago.

"I would ask you how you are feeling," she said, "but I know how I felt being the victim of a gunshot wound."

"Yes, I imagine you do. This is like reverse *déjà vu*. I recall coming to visit you in this same hospital."

"How crazy is that? I could laugh, but the thought of me and you getting shot isn't funny."

"Your case is a little different from mine."

Megan looked thoughtful. "The scene in front of city hall the day with Tracy reminded me of my situation years ago, except Danny took the shot meant for her."

Pain pierced through me as I tried to sit up. Megan's expression mirrored my distress. She quickly moved closer to the bed.

"Don't try to get up. Let me see if I can raise the head of your bed a little." She pressed a button on the remote.

A whirring sounded as my upper body raised with the bed. "That's good. Thanks."

She sat in the chair and crossed her legs. "Can you tell me anything about what's happening with this case y'all are working on with Danny?"

"I'm not sure if I can without you being my attorney. At the moment, I don't need legal help." My gaze met hers. "Believe me, I would love to confide in you about this case, but you *are* a defense attorney."

A frown wrinkled her forehead. "Susan, you know good and well I would never agree to represent a person who had caused harm to a member of my family. I couldn't do it ethically, much less legally."

I averted my eyes for a moment. "What's wrong with me? I'm talking nonsense. I didn't mean to insult you. I'm frustrated that I can't do anything." I motioned with my head toward my injury. "Even Danny no longer has to wear his arm sling."

She waved my apology away. "And I didn't mean to get on my high horse. Let's chalk it up to the craziness of the whole situation."

"Deal."

"I really wanted to help with the case if I could. This business has gotten a lot more serious since Danny got shot. Your shooting and Tracy's kidnapping has amped the situation up two more notches. I don't know how I could help, but if there's anything you need, I'm here."

"There is something you can do." I eyed her with caution. "I need to get your advice about a dream."

"A dream?"

"Well, perhaps a better description would be a drug-induced vision."

Her eyes widened. "Now you've got my curiosity piqued."

"Experts say your dreams are indicative of your subconscious."

She agreed. "That's what I learned in psychology class in college, but I don't claim to be any kind of authority on the subject."

I cleared my throat. "Let me give you a little backstory. Last year after Josh and I decided to start dating, I had a short dream in which Jim made this statement, 'You're going to be okay.' At the time, I didn't sit down and try to analyze what his message might mean."

I studied her face. No overt reaction. "Today, after the nurse gave me a relaxant, he came to me again with the same message. When I asked how this could be, he added, 'without me.'"

I explained the rest of my vision, including the part about Josh. She remained silent for what seemed like a long time. I began to wonder if she intended to comment.

"Sounds like Jim is giving you permission to move on with your life. With Josh...perhaps?" she added. "Speaking of Josh...what's going on between you two? I know that's none of my business, but I could see the situation up here didn't seem right. I expected him to be sitting here by your bedside."

"You're right. Guess I overreacted to his remarks."

"What happened?"

I described his delay in informing me of his meeting with Dave Falcon and the rest of our conversation. "Am I overreacting, or is he?"

She steepled her fingers for a short moment. "That's a hard one, but here goes. In my opinion, you both reacted excessively to the situation."

I frowned. "How?'

"In your mind, Josh's remarks were disrespectful of Jim and your feelings for Jim."

"He should know I'll always have affection or even love for Jim, but that doesn't mean I can't love another man," I said.

"Yes, he should know. Believe it or not, men have extremely fragile egos. Even big strong men. To Josh, Falcon told him he'd never measure up to Jim. And let's face it. Jim would be a hard act to follow in Josh's mind. Not only for him, but for Matthew too."

"That's what Josh basically said about never measuring up. What about my part? What could I have said differently?"

"I understand your feelings, especially since he waited so long to tell you about his meeting. You're in a difficult position because of Matthew. He may be unhappy and still upset about Jim's death and Josh's presence in your life. But he's a child."

Spoken like a woman who has no children, I thought. *Oh dear. Isn't that what I said to Josh?*

"I'm sure Josh would never do anything to hurt Matthew or Caroline," she continued. "He could be a great role model, but you deserve happiness also. If Josh makes you happy and you want to make this relationship permanent, then the two of you need to talk about everything, including Matthew."

The door to my room opened and Rachel walked in. "I know Doctor Theriot said only one visitor at a time, but I have a little bit of news." She frowned. "Not that great news, however."

I tried to lean forward but a twinge of pain stopped me. "Don't keep us hanging."

"Tracy's car has been found parked two blocks from the cemetery."

My heart sank. "But no sign of her?"

"I'm afraid not."

"Megan, if Tracy makes it out...alive, she may need your services as a defense attorney."

Twenty-four

The two women stared at me in surprise. I clasped my hand over my mouth.

"What do you mean?" Megan stood and moved closer to the bed.

Rachel raised her eyebrows. "Should I leave?"

"I shouldn't have said anything. I did tell Danny, but I assume he didn't reveal that part."

"He only said she had been kidnapped," Rachel said.

"We should leave the conversation there." Eyeing Megan I said, "If the need arises, would you be available to take her on as a client?"

"Of course. Is there a big chance this could happen?"

"I don't know how much of a chance there is for her to need your services. Something she said to me directly before those two guys showed up makes me believe she might."

"I wish you wouldn't have mentioned this at all," Megan remarked.

I shook my head. "So do I."

"Now, Rachel and I will be wondering about this all night."

"My curiosity might get the best of me," Rachel agreed. "I'm going to bug Danny until he tells me."

"Don't you dare." If she went through with her actions, Danny would most likely know the origin of the information. "I always open my big mouth when I shouldn't." I looked at each of the women. "If Danny wants to reveal what I told him, that's fine, but we don't even know if Tracy is still alive. Her remarks might be moot."

"True enough. I believe I'll say goodbye for now." Megan clasped my hand for a short moment. "I'll come back to see you soon."

"I hope you'll be seeing me back at my house sooner rather than later."

"I expect nothing less. I know you can't wait to get out of here."

"Absolutely."

"Steven is back in the waiting room," Rachel said. "I'll walk out with you and let him come in to visit."

Feeling helpless, I watched the two women leave. Tired of visitors, I wanted to go home. I chided myself for acting like a child. *Seems like all I do lately. I need to try and talk Doctor Theriot into releasing me from the hospital tomorrow. Talk to him like an adult, not a child throwing a tantrum.*

My brother walked nonchalantly into my room and plopped down in the chair Megan had vacated. "You're a lot calmer than the last time I saw you."

"Calmer, but a lot more frustrated."

"Yeah, you were ready to get out of here yesterday," he joked. "Even if you didn't realize it."

"You know me too well."

Steven narrowed his eyes. "Megan seemed preoccupied when she left your room. Are you two hatching one of your crazy plans?"

"No, we aren't. I opened my big mouth when I shouldn't have. Guess you could say I jumped the gun. Megan's probably trying to figure out how she can find out the reason for my slip of the tongue."

"Let me get this straight," Steven mused. "You spoke out of turn and didn't tell her the rest of the story?"

"That's about right. Danny might be mad at me for saying what I did. If he didn't tell any of you himself, then he didn't want the information out in public."

"He told us about the two men kidnapping Tracy and that one of the men shot you. Did you recognize one or both of them? He said you didn't."

"That's correct. I didn't recognize either one of them. They both wore masks. What I said to Megan concerned Tracy."

He didn't comment further about Tracy. "When you first came to, you were really in a state. Is there a reason other than you had experienced a traumatic event only hours ago?"

I glared at him. Although I shouldn't have. Like on other occasions, he sensed my distress involved a combination of reasons. "Did Josh tell you about what happened between us?"

"He indicated y'all had an argument, but didn't go into detail. After we were run out of your room, I figured a few things out. Correct me if I'm wrong. Your emotions were running wild when you left the house after the argument, so what happened at the cemetery really sent you into a tailspin. You didn't want to be deterred by anybody." He tilted his head slightly to one side.

I blew out a long breath. "As usual, you are straight on."

He grinned. "My 'twin-stinct' is always on target."

I rolled my eyes. "But you're correct in your assessment of my situation. I need a man's point of view. I told Megan and got her opinion."

"About your argument with Josh?"

"Yes." Steven agreed to hear me out. I proceeded to tell him about our conversation regarding Josh's meeting with Dave Falcon.

"What do you think? Did I overreact?"

He studied my face for a short moment. "You did overreact, in a way. I think you've probably been showing signs, anticipating the anniversary of Jim's death."

I started to object, but he interrupted. "Let me finish. You might not have even realized you were thinking about the event. I believe Josh noticed, but figured everything would get back to normal after the date passed."

"That still doesn't explain why he waited so long to tell me about meeting Dave Falcon."

"I know how I would feel in his situation. This is my guess. When Falcon started singing Jim's praises, his ego got bruised. Falcon's praise for Jim may have been exaggerated in Josh's mind since he had noticed your actions prior to his trip. Frankly, I can't figure out why Falcon would have been praising Jim to Josh's face anyway."

"I couldn't imagine why either. Maybe he doesn't like Josh. You know some cops don't like private investigators."

Steven gave a sarcastic laugh. "Yet *he's* become one of those disliked private investigators."

"True. So if that's Falcon's reason for speaking the way he did to Josh, he's a big hypocrite, so let me get this straight," I continued. "You believe the combination of events made Josh start feeling like he could never measure up to Jim with me?"

"That's about it. You'll have to talk things over with Josh and tell him in a calm conversation what your position is about your relationship with him. That is, if you still want a relationship with him."

"Funny, you and Megan gave me the same advice, even though your words were a little different from hers." I didn't speak for a long moment. "I need to think about what I want for me and for the kids. Would you mind leaving me alone for a while?"

He stood and walked over to the bed. "Okay, try to get some rest. I'll check in with you later." He leaned over and kissed me on the forehead.

I watched him walk out the door. A feeling of loneliness crept over me. What did I want? I had a lot to consider. I couldn't second guess myself.

As soon as I started sifting through all the events of the past few days, I had one interruption after another. Nurses checking IVs. Aides taking blood pressure.

Finally, Doctor Theriot walked into the room. Then it occurred to me: The only way to get my thoughts and my life straightened out would be to convince him I needed to be released from the hospital.

He might not agree. But what did I have to lose?

Twenty-five

Monday, July 21

I felt relieved at being able to go home. Doctor Theriot didn't have the same feeling about releasing me, especially since I more or less vowed to leave whether he released me or I checked out myself. Rachel came to my rescue and promised him she would make sure I'd keep out of trouble. Of course, Rachel drove. No driving for me yet. Come to think of it, I wouldn't mind being chauffeured around town for a short time. But only a short time.

"When are the kids coming home?" Rachel asked.

"Next week on Wednesday." My stomach clenched. "What's the date today?"

"The twenty first. Why...? Never mind. I know why you asked. Tomorrow is the anniversary of Jim's death."

"I wanted to go to his grave, but under the circumstances that's not a good idea." My lip trembled. I forced myself not to cry.

"You're right. It's not a good idea." She reached over and patted me on the arm. "Maybe we can come up with our own ceremony tomorrow."

Rachel turned the car into her driveway and cut the engine. She gave me that "I'm the boss so you will obey me" look.

"What?"

"You will be recuperating in our guest room for as long as it takes," she said.

I wanted to be in my own bed, but I knew she had no intention of allowing me to be alone in my house. "I agree, on one condition. I am not going to be treated as an invalid. No nightgowns or PJs except at night."

An amused look crossed her face. "Agreed. The first sign of any discomfort or unusual pain and Doctor Theriot will get a call."

I rolled my eyes. "Yes, Mother. I promise to follow your orders."

She gave me a thumbs up. "Good girl."

I couldn't help laughing at our silly exchange. Releasing even a part of the tension I'd experienced lately felt good.

"After I get settled, I intend to continue reading Harriet's journal. There's no telling what other goodies might be hidden in there."

"Good idea," Rachel said. "I've been wanting to look into Anne LeBlanc's diary again. Now let's go inside."

As I exited the car, I suddenly thought about my cat. "What about Katy? Has anyone checked on her?"

"Don't worry," Rachel assured me. "We have taken good care of her. Actually, Remi even went over there one day to feed her and play with her."

"Wow! She seems to have forgotten about the cat who jumped in the crib to suffocate the baby."

Rachel and I both laughed.

A sharp pain pierced my shoulder. I grimaced. "Supposedly laughing is good for the soul, but the movement involved isn't so great for a gunshot wound."

"It'll get better," she said and motioned for me to follow her inside the house.

"I'll have to go easy on the laughter for a while."

"You simply have to take it easy. I'd hate for you not to laugh at all until you're healed."

"Yeah, what if I don't heal," I groaned.

Rachel glared at me. "Don't you dare start thinking about such foolishness. You are going to heal." She brought my sparse belongings into the guest bedroom. "We can go over to your house later and pick up more of your clothes."

"Sure, that's fine." I suddenly felt down, mentally and physically. "I need to rest for a while. All this movement has taken more out of me than I anticipated."

An expression of concern flitted across Rachel's face. She quickly changed her expression and smiled. "You've had surgery and been off your feet for days, all the result of a traumatic event. This is a normal reaction."

I leaned back onto the fluffy pillows. Rachel retrieved a light blue throw blanket from the back of a chair and spread it over me.

"I'll check on you after a while," she said and closed the door behind her.

I shut my eyes and dozens of images and questions flipped through my mind. What was I going to do about Josh? I missed his company.

Both Megan and Steven seemed to be advising me to get back together with him. At least that's the impression I got from both of them. Maybe I'd only imagined they were counseling me to reunite with Josh because subconsciously I wanted to do so. I had to make up my own mind after he and I hashed everything out.

Other questions preyed on my mind concerning Tracy's kidnapping. Who were those men? Why did they take her and shoot me?

And the most important question about Tracy...Was she still alive?

Twenty-six

I awoke with a start. Where was I? Then I remembered. Rachel's guest room. Exhaling deeply, I pushed myself up from the pillows.

An ache in my shoulder sparked a groan. I had a few choices. Take a pain pill and fall asleep again. Suck it up and endure the pain, or take OTC pain meds. I opted for the OTC. Rachel probably had what I needed in her medicine cabinet.

After moving my legs to the side of the bed, I attempted to stand. My legs felt rubbery. I never thought surgery on my shoulder would make my legs weak. But then I'd never had real surgery. My only experience with any procedure remotely like an operation might have been giving birth to twins. Guess that's close enough, I thought, recalling the event nine years ago.

At that moment I began to believe getting shot had messed up my brain. My strange statements, blurting out information, and almost insulting Megan didn't seem like me. My previous thoughts had been scrambled.

I remembered a statement Jim made years ago concerning a police officer being shot and his partner shooting a suspect. Both men had to receive a psychological evaluation and therapy in order to return to work. *Will I need to have psychotherapy?*

I walked to the door at a snail's pace and stepped into the hall. I found Rachel in the kitchen.

She pulled a chair away from the table and motioned for me to sit. "Would you like something to eat?"

"I don't feel like eating," I said, sinking into the chair. With my arm in a sling to take the pressure off my shoulder, I felt out of balance and almost missed the chair.

She frowned. "You need to get food into your body to get your strength back."

"Sorry, I must sound like an obstinate child. You're right, of course." I eyed her with hesitancy. "When I first awoke, I started thinking that I might need therapy. My thoughts seem scrambled and I've blurted out statements, things I shouldn't have said."

Rachel studied me for a while before speaking. "Many people have side-effects from the anesthetic. I think that's what may be happening. Food and rest are the cure. As far as the therapy is concerned, a few sessions with a psychologist might be in order later to help you get over the trauma of being shot, but don't rush into that option."

I gave a weak smile. "Agreed. What's on the menu?"

Rachel prepared a bowl of tomato soup and a grilled cheese sandwich for me. Those comfort foods usually are considered a great winter combo, but I think the duo is wonderful any time of the year. That is, except in summer when your A/C is broken. Then I would opt for a snowball, one of those delicious local treats made with crushed ice topped with any flavor of syrup over the top.

"I must admit, I feel better since eating," I said. "In fact, if you don't have other plans, we should walk over to my house and gather a few items for me. I'll be able to have some time with Katy. I hate for her to be all alone over there."

"We can bring her over here, if you'd like," Rachel suggested. "She won't be any trouble."

I agreed. Fifteen minutes later, she and I walked across to my house.

The house phone rang immediately after we entered. I answered with a curt hello. Probably one of those robo-scams wanting me to buy an extended warranty on my car.

The woman's voice on the other end sounded live, not recorded. "We didn't intend to kill you this time. Only to scare you. Next time you might not be so lucky." The line went dead.

Rachel frowned. "Who was that?"

When my heartbeat slowed to a somewhat normal rate, I answered. "I don't know, but a woman threatened me."

"Let me see the phone number." Rachel moved closer to check the caller ID. She turned to me, her jaw tightening. "Just our luck, the number's blocked."

"I don't remember if that other call I received had the number blocked. The call surprised me. I didn't think to check it out."

"You mean the one both you and Remi received the same day?"

"Yes, that's the one."

"Maybe Remi may still have a record of that on her phone. I'll check with her later. Oh, I almost forgot. She called earlier to check on you. She said she'd get back later today."

A soft meow caught my attention. Katy ran to me and rubbed against my legs. "I suppose you need either food or TLC or both," I said to her as if she could answer.

She looked up at me and issued a loud meow, then turned and ran toward the kitchen.

"There's your answer," Rachel said. "The TLC can come later."

We sat for a while at the kitchen table while Katy ate the food I'd delivered to her bowl. I thought back to the woman's threat. "I don't know if this means anything or not. The woman on the phone didn't mention Tracy's kidnapping."

Rachel looked thoughtful. "She only referred to your shooting. Perhaps she wanted to get off the phone as quickly as possible."

"That could be," I said. "I believe there's some other reason."

"Like what?"

"I don't know yet. Maybe I'm grasping at straws, but I can't help feeling what she didn't say might be an important clue to what happened at the cemetery."

Twenty-seven

I needed...and wanted to phone Josh to talk about our situation. I stalled. Would he even answer my call?

After speaking with Steven and Megan concerning the problem, I understood how Josh must have felt. Like Megan said, in Josh's mind, Jim would be a hard act to follow, especially if I'd given him that impression. Would this situation be repeated with any man I decided to date?

There was only one way to find out what the future held. I keyed Josh's number on my cell phone. His voice mail picked up after four rings.

"Josh, it's Susan," I said, feeling and most likely sounding awkward. "Please give me a call. I...we need to talk." Now if only he would return my call.

My phone rang and startled me. The number shown on the caller ID proved disappointing.

"Hi, Dad," I said. "What's up?"

"You know very well what's up. Why didn't you tell us you had been shot?" His voice sounded a lot different from his usual laid-back tone.

"I'm sorry. I didn't want to worry you and Mother. Steven must have given you the news. I'm at Rachel's house taking it easy and I expect to make a full recovery."

"Yes, Steven did tell us about the event. I'm glad Rachel is there to make sure you do take it easy." He paused for a long moment. "Your mother wants to speak to you."

"Dad, I'm not in the mood for her condemnations." I clenched my teeth. "Simply tell her I'm on the mend and she has nothing to worry about."

"Susan," he began. "I know you don't like her reprimands, but she is your mother. I'm putting her on the phone."

I blew out a deep breath. She didn't immediately come on the line. A muffled conversation ensued. Finally, I heard her voice.

"How are you feeling?" she asked.

"A little bit of pain in my shoulder, that's all. Doctor Theriot says I'll be fine in about a week or so. I have an appointment next week for a follow-up."

"Your father says you're staying at Rachel's. I do hope you'll follow her instructions and the doctor's orders."

There it is. Very subtle. She's working up to her usual routine.

"I promise I'll follow everyone's orders. Don't worry. I'll be fine."

"How can I not worry about you with your crime solving business?" She sniffed. "It's so dangerous."

"Sometimes it is dangerous. But it's what I enjoy doing. I'm not a child. Now I'm getting tired, so I have to get off the phone."

"You may be an adult, but your children aren't. I don't approve of your dangerous lifestyle choices," she said with a huff.

That did it. "Mother, I'm sorry for being rude, but you have never approved of any decision I've ever made, including my marriage to Jim. Right now, I can't deal with your admonishments. Goodbye."

My father returned to the phone. "I'll call you again soon. Then I'll relay the update on your condition to her so you won't have to speak to her."

"Thanks, Dad. You must think I'm a horrible daughter for speaking to Mother like that, but like I told her, she has never approved of any decision I've ever made."

"I know she can be difficult, so I understand your position. I love you."

"Love you too." We ended the call with me feeling remorseful about the way I had spoken to Mother. Her remark about my children had felt like a stab in the chest. I would never forgive myself if anything happened to them because of my actions.

Dad had hit the nail on the head when he said Mother could be difficult. I suppose she'd always meant well, but she and I lived in two different worlds. When Steven and I were born, her marriage to Dad meant she could give us all the advantages she'd never had growing up. Parents can't live their lives through their children, though. Children shouldn't be forced to take piano lessons or play baseball simply because their parents always wanted to, but missed out on in their own youth.

My phone rang and interrupted my mental rant about parents. This time the caller was Josh. My heartbeat accelerated. "Hi, I'm glad you called me back."

"I'm glad you called," he said. "How are you doing? You had a pretty serious wound."

"Depending on how I move, my shoulder hurts, but otherwise I'm doing okay." An uncomfortable silence ensued. "Josh, I would like very much to see you. We need to talk about what happened between us."

"I agree. Is there some place private we can talk?"

"We can get together at my house, if that's okay with you. I'm staying with Rachel and Danny for the time being, but I'm up and around, so it's no problem for me to walk across the yard."

"Can we meet in about an hour?"

I agreed and we ended the call. Would this meeting be a new beginning for us? Or the beginning of the end?

Twenty-eight

I informed Rachel about my meeting with Josh and walked across the yard to my house. My stomach felt queasy after my angry response to Mother's reproach. Meeting with Josh so soon after that phone call wasn't doing anything for my state of mind either.

I spotted Harriet Haydel's journal atop the kitchen table where I had left it Saturday. Maybe delving into the book again would keep my mind occupied until Josh arrived. I had no idea what I would say to him or vice versa.

Katy brushed against my legs and meowed softly. "Hi, girl," I said. "Surprised to see me again so soon? After a while, you can come with me to Rachel's house."

She tilted her head lightly to one side. Her confused expression seemed to ask, "When is this household getting back to normal?"

"I wish I knew. Maybe this is the new normal." I managed to scoot a chair away from the table and sat, almost losing my balance in the process. I knew how Danny must have felt with his arm in a sling. Luckily, mine was on my left arm. You never realize how much you rely on your left hand and arm for certain actions, even if you are right-handed.

I turned the pages of Harriet's journal and picked up where I had left off on Saturday. For months her entries contained descriptions of the weather and other mundane topics like everyday activities needed to run a plantation. I found no further mention of Charles' illegitimate son with Mya the Burmese nanny until Christmas Eve of nineteen twenty-nine.

Christmas Eve turned out to be one of those balmy December days not uncommon in Louisiana. I met with the cook to prepare the menu for dinner this evening. I happened to glance out the window and observed Chun seated on a blanket in the garden with Ruth having a "pretend" tea party. Lying next to Chun, the boy, now almost five months old, hugged a stuffed bear. I looked away quickly as he reminded me of Charles' betrayal.

What had this poor child been named? Further reading indicated Harriet always referred to him as "the boy." A knock at the door interrupted my trip back in history.

Josh and I stared at each other for a short moment. "I'm sorry," he and I said at the same time.

I ushered him into the kitchen, feeling slightly awkward. "Have a seat. Coffee?"

"Yeah, I could use some. You need help?"

"No, I'm fine." *I'm really not, but not willing to admit how shaky I'm feeling.*

Seeing Josh again made me realize what had gone wrong. In my mind, I had been comparing him to Jim without even realizing it. If I ever wanted to move on with Josh, I couldn't continue causing him to feel like he had a ghost for a rival.

Jim had given me permission to move on with my love life and life in general. I needed to give myself permission. Doing so proved not to be as easy as it sounded.

"After I heard about your shooting, I stewed about everything that happened between us," he said, taking a seat at the table. He didn't elaborate further, then changed the subject. "You're looking good. Leaving the hospital to recover must be what it takes."

"You said it. I hate hospitals. It seems I always end up in one because I get in trouble snooping around where I don't belong. Except this time, I happened to be minding my own business." *Sort of, anyway.*

I poured coffee into the two cups, but realized I couldn't carry both to the table at the same time.

Josh stood. "Here, you sit and I'll get the coffee."

After setting the cups in front of us, he returned to his chair. He glanced at the table for a short moment. "I'm sorry for not telling you about Dave Falcon. I don't know why I let him get to me. He probably didn't have any intention of putting me down."

"You're not completely at fault. Apparently, I've given you a reason to doubt yourself and our relationship." I studied his face to try and discern his feelings. Was he going to give me an answer about my actions? He seemed hesitant to speak his mind.

"I noticed a number of times you seemed distant," he finally said. "The closer the anniversary of Jim's death came, the more times you were not here in spirit." His steady gaze unnerved me.

"The day Jim died devastated me. The anniversary brings back those memories."

"Why didn't you talk to me about what you were feeling?"

"I didn't think you would appreciate hearing me talk about Jim."

He didn't speak for what seemed like a long time. "And my reaction to Dave Falcon's remarks must have proved your suspicions. I guess you felt I had disrespected you and the love you felt for Jim."

"Disrespect is an overused word these days. At the time, your words did offend me. I couldn't understand why you suddenly felt unsure of our relationship. In hindsight, not talking to you about my anxiety for the approaching anniversary seems foolish.

"I loved Jim, but that doesn't mean I can't ever love another man," I continued. "I know there are problems with Matthew, but I hoped we could get through those issues together. Is there any possibility we can start over?"

His expression lightened. "Anything's possible. I'm ready to try if you are." He held out his hand.

I smiled and reached out to take it. "I am."

Suddenly I felt as exhausted as if I had run a marathon. Apparently, Josh picked up on my physical condition before I had a chance to cut our meeting short.

"You probably need to get some rest," he said, brushing my cheek with his hand. "Surgery is nothing to mess around with. I'll walk you back to Rachel's house."

"I may have overdone things emotionally and physically on my first day home from the hospital. Before you arrived, I had a very angry conversation with my mother. And then, anticipating our talk didn't do much for my peace of mind. While you were on your way over here, I felt anxious about how this meeting would turn out."

"You were already upset before I arrived? I'm glad I didn't know about the phone call with your mom. I would've been even more nervous." He gave a faint smile. "I have the impression you and your mom don't get along."

"Long story," I said. "After I get back my strength, I'll fill you in on our history and other events in my past."

"That's fine. You need to get off your feet and relax for now."

"If I tell you the story about my relationship with my mother, I need something in return."

He raised an eyebrow. "What do you need?"

"If we're both going to communicate more about our difficulties and our feelings, you need to tell me about *your* past, such as your life in Jennings. My feeling is there are a lot of emotions involved with your time there."

"That's only fair," he said.

I eyed him for a short moment. "There's something else. Mother made a remark about the twins which I can't ignore. She suggested that my lifestyle placed them in danger. This is a problem I must consider if I continue to work with you at your office. So, that's a subject we need to explore together."

"We still have a lot to discuss. Until next time." He planted a kiss on my lips.

Twenty-nine

With Anne Richard LeBlanc's journal in hand, Rachel settled onto the sofa in their living room, a part of the house rarely used except for large gatherings. The quiet here would be good for her concentration. Danny had left the house earlier with Ronnie to check out some information an informant had relayed concerning Tracy's possible location.

She reviewed Anne's family line in her mind. Anne's mother Ruth was the daughter of Charles and Harriet Haydel. She'd married Michael Richard. In 1963, Anne married Carl LeBlanc and Melanie, the main cold case victim, was their daughter.

Whew, she thought. *This could get complicated.* But family connections always seem to be complicated.

Anne had begun keeping this journal a few years before her marriage. The pages were filled with descriptions of fancy social events and debutante cotillions. Then came the big wedding in June of 1963. The guest list included all of Cypress Lake's wealthy residents, along with New Orleans society bigwigs and Lafayette socialites. In Anne's words, "Everyone who is anyone in South Louisiana."

Rachel thumbed through pages, hoping to find a clue concerning the so-called hit-and-run accident that took Anne's life. Nothing of interest turned up at first., but an entry two months after Anne's marriage to Carl LeBlanc suddenly caught her eye.

August 2, 1963

I am furious, plus my heart is broken. I discovered Carl has been cheating on me since even before we married. I saw him helping her out of our boat at the dock. In plain sight. Our boat! They looked pretty cozy. My friend Jeanette Carson admitted she'd known about the affair long before Carl and I married. Some friend. She could have warned me about Maddie Lagarde.

August 3, 1963

I confronted Carl about his boat ride with Maddie. He blew me off, saying the incident didn't mean anything except a boat ride with a friend. I told him in no uncertain terms that I wouldn't stand for his infidelity. If he wanted to be with her, why did he marry me? For my money, of course.

"Money is always a good motive for murdering your wife," Rachel said out loud. "Or to have her murdered."

She closed the journal to give her eyes a break. Her mind wandered to Susan and her meeting with Josh. She hoped everything would work out favorably. Although tempted to get up and peek out the window, she knew that would be spying. Susan hadn't confided in her about the subject of their disagreement, so how serious the argument was or what any misunderstanding might have been she didn't know.

In her mind Josh and Susan made a perfect pair. *Darn it. That's not my choice to make.* She brushed off those reflections, but her thoughts turned to Tracy Lassiter's plight and the journals written by Tracy's grandmother and great-grandmother. Could Tracy's mother Melanie have continued the tradition and written her own diary? She made a mental note to ask Danny about such an item. If there turned out to be another journal, perhaps there would be a clue to the identity of her killer.

Rachel reopened Anne's journal, hoping a juicy item or clue would jump out at her. At the moment, locating important information didn't seem probable. For several years, Anne wrote sparingly, not every day. She had made an entry to note the birth of Melanie, her only child, in 1965. She added that Carl had expressed disappointment because the baby didn't turn out to be a boy.

After that entry, the pages either were blank or regarding a mundane activity. Rachel started to lose the hope of finding any clue about what might have caused Anne's murder. Then an entry written less than a year before her death caught her eye.

July 4, 1973

I met him at our annual party. Besides being handsome and intelligent, Phillip paid attention to me. I definitely enjoyed his company. I didn't have contact with Carl until early morning, when the festivities ended and I went up to bed. Drunk out of his mind, he had passed out on our bed. The covers were a mess. I'd bet my last dollar Maddie sneaked up here with him. She definitely didn't make the guest list, so he smuggled her or another one of his trashy women up to our bed.

Something sparkly caught my eye next to one of the pillows. I discovered a gold dangle earring, oval shaped with a small ruby in the center. Was this gem real or only glass? Seeing the red jewel brought to mind the story passed down through the generations about a large ruby Grandfather Haydel brought back from Burma. As a child, I remember hearing about the curse of the ruby from those Wilson kids and even some of their parents. Whoever owned the gem had a curse put on them. I personally have never laid eyes on the ruby. No one knew where Grandfather had put it for safekeeping, but our family must still be in possession of the stone because we do seem to be cursed.

The next few pages told of secret meetings with Phillip. Rachel figured Carl LeBlanc may have discovered Anne's trysts with another man. There's the old double standard rearing its head, she thought. Perfectly fine for Carl to have a mistress, but not a lover for Anne.

She heard Danny come inside the house and call out to her. "In here," she answered.

He appeared in the doorway. He didn't look happy when he sat on the sofa next to her.

"No luck finding clues on Tracy's kidnapping, I gather," she said, closing the journal.

"Not a total loss. Our informant happened to be walking past the back gate of the cemetery and saw Tracy being hustled into the white pickup. He didn't recognize the men, but gave a description. Ronnie and I went back over the area in the cemetery to see if we'd missed any evidence."

Rachel perked up. "Did you find anything?"

"There were a few cigarette butts and an empty soft drink can. We collected those items to be tested for DNA. But who knows if they were there when we last searched the area." He shrugged. "I don't want to get my hopes up too high. The cigarette butts and the can were not together in one spot."

"Earlier today, Susan and I went over to her house to collect some of her clothes," Rachel said. "She got another one of those threatening phone calls."

Danny raised his eyebrows. "Man or woman?"

"A woman. She told Susan they'd only wanted to scare her, not kill her by shooting her. But she threatened to finish the job if Susan didn't leave well enough alone. The woman didn't mention Tracy's kidnapping, and Susan seemed to think that meant something."

"Like what?"

"Susan didn't come right out and say it, but this is my take on a possible meaning. The woman didn't know about Tracy, only that Susan had been shot. She wanted her group to take credit for the shooting."

"Possible, I suppose." Danny looked thoughtful for a short moment. "In that case, there could be two different groups of people who don't want us to find out who killed Melanie or her mother."

"And maybe the men who kidnapped Tracy and shot Susan are different from the person who shot at you and Tracy," Rachel said. "Whoever these people are, I suspect they all must be trying to get possession of that ruby, regardless of the curse or whoever stands in their way."

Thirty

Tuesday, July 22

I never imagined surgery would leave me so tired. I never want to have another one. Yesterday I had forgotten my promise to Katy to take her over to Rachel's house. As I drifted off to sleep last night, I remembered, but felt too weak to do anything.

To my surprise, Katy lay snuggled next to me this morning. Rachel, bless her heart, had brought the cat and all her belongings and placed them in the room. I did not wake up the whole time this went on. I must be totally worn out.

Today would be different. I'd take it easy. Read more of Harriet Haydel's journal. I had the feeling there would be surprising information.

"Oh, no," I said out loud. Today marked the second anniversary of Jim's death. I wanted to commemorate the day in some way. Due to my condition, going to the cemetery would not be a good idea. There could also be a danger from the men who shot me and kidnapped Tracy. Although the odds of that happening were not high unless I went there by myself, which I had no intention of doing. In a way, I wished the twins could be here with me to honor their father, but I had the feeling their presence at any type of memorial would cause more emotional distress for them.

My stomach growled. I needed food. My brain would be better able to make a decision about honoring Jim after I had breakfast.

An hour later, I had made a decision about how to honor Jim's memory. Rachel and I had discussed all the possibilities available to me under the circumstances.

I decided not to have a ceremony or anything resembling a memorial service. I planned to take some time to myself and say prayers for Jim. Maybe even 'speak' to him. Then, I would go about my day as normal.

As I had told myself a number of times in the last few days, Jim had given me permission to move on with my life. I had to give *myself* permission. That's exactly what I intended to do. In my mind, the best option seemed to be going full time with my writing. Of course, I could always help Josh by taking care of any paperwork associated with his office. There would be time to make those decisions after I'd recovered my strength.

Later in the afternoon, I retrieved Harriet Haydel's journal from my house and sat on the bed in Rachel's guest room. She followed me in, holding the journal of Anne Richard LeBlanc and sat in a small flowered upholstered chair close to the bed.

"Oh, yes," I said. "You told me you had discovered interesting events. Tell me about what you found."

"It seems Carl LeBlanc had an affair even before he and Anne married, and continued to see this woman afterwards. Then years later, shortly before her death, Anne met a man named Phillip with whom she started an affair."

I widened my eyes. "Goodness. What a soap opera. Maybe those shows really do reflect real life."

"Especially among the rich and famous, which most characters are on those shows," Rachel added. "Anything interesting in Harriet's journal?"

"Did I tell you about the death in childbirth of Mya, one of the Burmese nannies?"

"I don't think so. A death in childbirth. One of the many so-called unexplained deaths attributed to the ruby's curse. I thought a blood family member would be the one who died."

"So did I. You'll never guess the identity of the baby's father. None other than Charles Haydel."

"Oh, my. What happened to the child?"

"He lived. Harriet turned over the boy to the other nannie to raise. She wrote that she couldn't bear to look at him because he reminded her of Charles' infidelity. In her later writings, she only referred to him as 'the boy.' Also, she said her time in Louisiana had caused her to lose her Christian values. She was too angry to forgive her husband and angry with God. This happened only a month after their daughter died in a horseback riding accident."

"Poor woman." Rachel looked thoughtful. "A woman's life historically has been in the hands of a man. First her father, then her husband. Death of women in childbirth and infant mortality were prevalent until way into the twentieth century."

"Modern women, at least in the U. S., are lucky. We do have a lot more freedom." I stared at the wall for a long moment. "I'm wondering exactly how angry Harriet was with Charles."

Rachel perked up. "Angry enough to push him off the balcony?"

I shrugged. "It's entirely possible."

"And Carl LeBlanc could very well have caused his wife's death. I need to read on and see if I can figure out if Carl discovered Anne's affair and decided to have her killed."

"There's still the curse of the ruby hanging over everyone in this family, even though they all seem to deny the story. I have the feeling such a tale would linger in the back of everyone's mind after each one of these terrible events." I mulled over my original idea about the power of suggestion to the cursed person, or in this case the cursed family. I asked Rachel for her opinion.

"Oh yes," she said. "All these deaths may have been deemed natural or accidental, even though there's more probable causes for murder, rather than a curse. In the subconsciouses of those who know the story about the stolen ruby, the power of suggestion would be strong."

"I'd also love to know where this ruby is located," I said. "Is it in a safe deposit box somewhere or hidden in the house in a secret room? Could someone have discovered it when they tore down the house?"

"If someone did find the ruby and is hiding it, or sold the valuable gem, that person could be perpetuating the curse myth and laughing all the way to the bank."

A thought came to me. "Or else Melanie LeBlanc's killer forced her to reveal the location of the gem before he killed her."

Thirty-one

Rachel and I continued reading the entries in the journals. Neither of us discovered any new information.

After hours of reading, my eyes were blurry. "I give up. There doesn't seem to be much hope of uncovering any more clues that might lead to the truth about all these deaths."

Rachel placed a hand on the back of her neck. "I agree. I've got a crick in my neck. Let's stop for a coffee break."

"Good idea."

We retired to the kitchen where Rachel started a fresh pot of coffee. A vehicle turning into the driveway caught my attention.

"That must be Danny," she said, retrieving a third mug from the cabinet.

A few minutes later he walked inside. I could tell by his pleased expression he had something new to report.

"Hello, ladies," he said. "A person of interest is back in town after an absence of about fifteen years."

Rachel automatically placed a cup of coffee on the table in front of an empty chair. Smiling like a cat who swallowed the canary, he sat down and looked at me and then Rachel.

"Come on," she said. "Don't keep us hanging."

I hate it when he keeps us guessing. "Okay, who is this person?"

"Brett Lassiter."

I did a double take. "Tracy's father?"

"Yeah, one and the same." He took a sip of coffee. "I didn't see him myself, but an informant reported seeing him at Bayou Pierre Bar two nights in a row last week. I think he said Wednesday and Thursday nights."

"Bayou Pierre Bar is one of those places you go if you don't want people to know you're in town," I noted.

He gave a harsh laugh. "Exactly."

"Why has he become a person of interest?" Rachel asked. "I thought he had an alibi for the night of Melanie's murder."

"He did. One we couldn't prove or disprove. Tracy reported that she phoned him sometime after she dialed nine-one-one. He didn't appear on the scene until after our units arrived. No blood or gunshot residue on him."

"So why has he become a person of interest?" I asked, repeating Rachel's question.

"Because Lassiter has men who work for him and he's not the kind of guy who would do the dirty work himself."

"What about his cell phone record? Did his phone ping off the right tower?"

"It did at his residence. However, he didn't live far from the crime scene at the time."

I narrowed my eyes. "Has he been notified about Tracy's kidnapping?"

Danny glared at me. "Why do I feel like I'm being interrogated?"

I shrugged. "Sorry. I got carried away."

"We didn't have current contact information on him," he continued. "I asked some of Ronnie's deputies to try to locate him, but they came up empty until now. I don't know all the details about how they were able to pinpoint his location. This came from one of the deputies' informants."

"Then we can safely assume Brett Lassiter still has acquaintances in town," I said. "People who informed him about Tracy."

Danny's cell phone rang and interrupted a reply. "Marchand." He responded positively to something the person on the other end said. "Good. Is he there now? ...Okay, I'll be down to the office in about fifteen minutes."

"I gather Brett Lassiter is at the sheriff's office," Rachel said to him.

"Yeah, Poche said Ronnie requested my presence during the interview."

Ten minutes later, Danny left the house for his talk with Brett Lassiter.

"Who is Poche?" I asked. "Is he new?"

"No, Johnny's been around for a while. He served in patrol for years at the Foretville substation. He's now Ronnie's chief deputy."

"If he spent his career at the Foretville substation, that's why I never heard of him." For a moment I felt an emptiness, reminding me I hadn't been completely in the loop since Jim died and Danny retired. I shook off the thought. "I wonder why the guys are using the term interview to tell Brett about Tracy."

Rachel shrugged. "Ronnie may have called him and asked him to come down to the station and didn't tell him why."

"In that case it wouldn't surprise me if he came accompanied by his attorney."

"Or else someone told him about Tracy's kidnapping and he wants to know why he wasn't informed," she added.

"I guess we'll find out what's going on a few hours from now." Patience was not one of my virtues. I'd sure love to be a fly on the wall in the interview room. "Oh, I just realized what Danny might have started to say. If Brett was seen in town last week, he should know about Tracy's kidnapping and my shooting from the newspaper report and Remi's TV interview with Ronnie."

"The article in the paper and Remi's TV piece didn't give any names. The sheriff's office 'declined to identify the victims at this time.'" She made air quotes to note her last words.

"Standard procedure. Oh well," I lamented. "Maybe he didn't know. So much for considering him as a suspect."

~ * ~

Danny eyed Brett Lassiter with both curiosity and suspicion. The look Lassiter gave him when he walked into the room suggested the man had the same feelings about him and Ronnie.

Lassiter frowned. "What's this all about? You said it concerned Tracy. Now what's going on? Is she in some kind of trouble?"

"Why would you think she was in trouble?" Ronnie asked.

Lassiter gave a shrug. "She got into a lot of trouble as a teenager. It's only natural to think that, especially with all this beating around the bush y'all are doing."

Danny leaned forward. "Actually, she is in trouble. She's been kidnapped."

He sat up straight. "When did this happen?"

"Last Saturday," Ronnie said. "The local paper had a write-up and TV news did a piece that night."

"I didn't hear anything about it. Why wasn't I notified?"

"Because nobody knew how to reach you," Danny said. "How long have you been back in town?"

Lassiter folded his arms. "Since Sunday night."

With his elbows resting on the table, Ronnie steepled his hands for a short moment. "What brings you back to town after all these years?"

Lassiter pounded his fist on the table. "Why are you asking me all these questions? I want to know about Tracy's kidnapping. Who the hell would want to take her?"

"That's what we're trying to figure out," Danny said. "Here's what we know. Two unidentified men grabbed her and one of them shot the person she had been talking to."

Lassiter seemed taken aback. Whether they were real or faked emotions, Danny couldn't determine. He had his doubts.

"The other person with Tracy...was she killed?"

Danny struggled to keep a stoic expression on his face. "No, only wounded." *We gave no mention of the sex of the wounded person in either newspaper or on TV. A slip of the tongue?*

Thirty-two

Josh came over later in the afternoon. Since Danny hadn't returned from the interview with Brett Lassiter, Rachel and I filled him in at the Marchands' kitchen table on everything we'd learned from the journals.

He looked thoughtful for a short moment. "Do you have the name of the mechanic who discovered the cut brake lines on Anne LeBlanc's car?"

"I don't recall offhand, but the receipt is in one of the folders we've been keeping on the family deaths."

I went back to the bedroom to retrieve the file. Upon returning to the kitchen, I pulled out the mechanic's note and read his name. "Jack...Broussard?" I eyed him with curiosity. "Broussard is pretty common in South Louisiana. Is he by some chance related to you?"

Josh raised an eyebrow and reached for the paper. "Let me see that." He gave a look of disbelief. "I don't normally believe in coincidences. However, in this case...he's my dad's first cousin and I know where to find him."

My mouth dropped open. "That is a coincidence."

"If Danny hasn't talked to him, I can get in touch with him and see what he remembers about the case."

"Danny probably hasn't spoken to him yet," Rachel said. "He's been working on the Melanie LeBlanc murder case and now on Tracy's kidnapping."

"Good, I'll give Jack a call and see what I can find out."

Ten minutes later, Danny returned from the sheriff's office. Rachel and I both looked at him expectantly. Josh greeted him with a handshake.

Danny exchanged a look with each one of us. "I guess y'all are waiting to hear about Brett Lassiter."

"Of course not," I said. "I'm certain the interview turned out to be boring, right?"

He gave a low chuckle, and then took a seat at the table. "We had to let him go. There wasn't anything to hold him on. There were some inconsistencies in his statements, though. He claimed to have only come into town Sunday evening."

"What about the informant's sighting of him at the bar?" Rachel asked.

"A case of mistaken identity, he claimed. We're having him tailed to see if we can find out what he's up to."

"Did he know about Tracy's kidnapping?" I asked. "And my shooting?"

"He said he didn't know. I told him basically what Remi's TV piece revealed. When I mentioned that the other person with Tracy had been shot, he seemed disturbed, but his reaction could have been faked. He asked about the person's condition. 'Was she killed?'"

"He said *she*? How did he know that if he got in town on Sunday?"

"Good question. I'm wondering why he came to town in the first place after being out of sight for years," Danny said. "You can bet he arrived long before he said."

"Maybe he came back after he heard about the reopening of his ex-wife's murder case." I calculated dates in my mind. "That would mean at least six or seven days."

Danny narrowed his eyes. "He's worried about what new evidence we might find to put him back on the suspect list."

"Yeah, if Lassiter did kill his wife, he made a risky move coming back to town now," Josh said. "He let his curiosity get the best of him. Dumb move."

Danny's laugh sounded more like a snort. "Nobody said criminals were smart."

I turned to Danny. "Remember the note from the mechanic about the brake lines being cut on Anne LeBlanc's car?"

He perked up at the mention of that case. "Yeah, what about him?"

"As it turns out, the mechanic is a cousin of Josh's."

"Whoa!" Danny exclaimed.

"No kidding," Josh said. "If you have no objection, I'd like to go talk to him to see what he remembers about that night."

"I don't have any problem with you talking to him. Is he still here in town?"

"No, he moved back to Jennings after he retired. At least that's the last I heard from family over there, but that's been a few years. I'll check and see if he's still living around there." He grimaced. "Or even if he's still alive."

"He was in his sixties at the time of Melanie's murder back in two thousand one," Danny said. "That would put him in his eighties today."

Josh considered that thought. "No telling what his health condition might be these days. I'd still like to give it a try anyway."

Danny agreed. "You never can tell what might come up."

Josh stepped into the living room to make his phone calls in private.

I wanted to accompany Josh on the drive to Jennings and started to ask, but after giving the idea some thought, I decided to wait until we were alone. I didn't want to put him on the spot in front of Danny and Rachel in case he had qualms about taking me along. There were various reasons he might not want me to come with him, including his secretiveness about growing up there and also the fact that I still needed recovery time from surgery. A nearly ten-hour round trip might be too tiring for me to handle at this point.

About twenty minutes later, he emerged from the other room with a strange look on his face. A look of anger, or shock, or determination. Maybe all three.

"I spoke to Jack's daughter, Adele. He had an accident in his truck last week and his injuries were too serious for the doctors to save him." He blew out a deep breath.

"Last week?" I couldn't believe it. "Another coincidence? You don't suppose his death was an accident?"

Rachel's expression suggested she thought my idea unrealistic. She started to comment, but Josh spoke up and all but confirmed my statement.

"Adele told me that Jack thought somebody had tailed him ever since he'd heard about Melanie LeBlanc's cold case being reopened. But the additional statement Danny made about evidence being tied to another family member's death made him jumpy."

I leaned forward in the chair. "Because he knew about the brake lines on Anne LeBlanc's car being cut and the authorities keeping that hush-hush."

"Adele also told me he'd mentioned some papers hidden in a closet. He told her about them before the accident and asked her to get a safe deposit box in her name to keep until the right person came along. She said, as he put it, 'or until you can get in touch with Ed's son.' Ed was my father," he added.

"So, are you going to Jennings?" I asked.

"Yeah, there could be valuable info in those papers." He glanced at Danny. "I don't know if there's a connection to Melanie's murder, but we might get lucky."

Thirty-three

I felt conflicted about asking to go to Jennings with Josh. The trip would be tiring for me so soon after surgery, which irked me to no end. When I find out who shot me and kidnapped Tracy, I'll do everything in my power to put that guy away.

Finally, I made the decision to at least ask him if I could accompany him to his old home town...as soon as we were alone. I began to wonder if being alone with him would ever happen today. People kept coming by, some to check on me, others to talk to Danny.

About six, Rachel started fiddling around in the kitchen as if trying to decide what to prepare for the evening meal.

Josh turned to me and asked in a low voice, "Do you feel up to going out to dinner with me?"

I smiled. "I'd love to. What did you have in mind?"

"Some place quiet so we can talk. Like Bijou's."

"That sounds nice. BB's it is."

Modeled after a small restaurant in Paris whose atmosphere the owner had visited and fallen in love with, the restaurant hadn't caught on at first. Some people even thought it was too fancy for Cypress Lake. Younger people decided against the place because no live music,

Cajun or otherwise, blasted through the doors. I enjoyed most music genres, except rap, but preferred elevator music while eating. *Wow, I must be getting old.*

Known to locals as Bijou's or sometimes BB's, the official name of the place, Bijou Bistro, fell by the wayside. Bijou's usually hosted a larger crowd on weekends, with reservations required. Weeknights were perfect for having a quiet conversation over a nice meal and a glass of wine.

An hour later, Josh and I walked into a dimly lit Bijou Bistro near the town of Foretville. The staff had turned down the lights for the evening meal. A single candle flickered in a glass bowl on each table.

Most of the people who patronized Bijou's were in their fifties, sixties, and older. Josh and I were probably some of the few younger ones to go there to eat. Only two of the six tables had guests enjoying the quiet, soothing atmosphere.

Although eating with a sling on my arm proved to be a bit awkward, the evening passed quickly. After a delicious meal, I sipped on my second glass of wine.

Josh leaned forward. "How do you feel about my taking another trip out of town?"

"I hope you're only going to be away for one day," I said. "Is there any reason to believe you would be in Jennings longer?"

He shrugged. "The last time I returned from out of town, I got in trouble with you."

I gave a faint smile. "I would hardly believe any person who knew Jim would be in Jennings. That's what started the whole affair."

"My insecurity, you mean?"

I grimaced. "I wasn't going to say that. What I meant was neither Jim nor I know anyone from there. I've never been to Jennings, and as far as I know, Jim hadn't either." I studied his face for a long moment in the flickering candlelight. "Actually, when the subject first came up, I wanted to ask if I could go with you."

He frowned. "Why didn't you say anything then?"

"I didn't want to put you on the spot in front of Danny and Rachel in case you didn't want me to go with you."

He tilted his head to one side and smiled. "I would love for you to come with me, but I'm worried the trip might be too tiring for you. Eight hours, round trip."

"I really wanted to see where you grew up," I groaned. *Quit sounding like a child, pouting because you didn't get your way.*

"This last week has been a trying time for you," he said. "There's nothing more traumatic than getting shot. Believe me, I know firsthand."

"It's also been a pretty upsetting week for you."

"Yes, it has, but most of the drama has been my own fault," he said. "When I return, I promise to tell you everything you want to know about my previous life. Sometime in the near future when you have fully recovered, we can take a trip there and you can meet the rest of my family."

"How many members of your family still live there?"

"Two sisters, a brother, and a few cousins." His expression clouded. "Both of my parents passed away years ago. I admit I haven't been back since Dad's funeral. He died a year after Mom."

I reached across the table and took his hand. "Then this would be the first time in a long time you've been to visit your family?"

"Except I won't be doing much visiting. I need to leave early so I can meet Adele at the bank to get those papers Jack left in her safe deposit box."

"Then we probably should get back to the house. I don't want you falling asleep at the wheel tomorrow."

Thirty-four

Wednesday, July 23

I couldn't believe how childish I had been about not being able to go along with Josh to Jennings. My previous idea of going to therapy returned to my mind. I remembered the times when I was hospitalized after being hit over the head by bad people. Could having too many hard knocks to the head be messing up my mind? Football players and other athletes who have head injuries end up with dementia, ALS and other assorted problems.

My phone rang and cut short my psychological self-diagnosis. I did a double take when I recognized the number on the ID display. Why would the camp director where the twins were staying be calling me?

"Hello." I thought my voice sounded as anxious as I felt. "This is Susan."

"This is Tom Carlson at your children's camp."

"Is everything okay? My kids..."

"No, no. Nothing physical happened to Matthew and Caroline." He paused for a long moment. "One of the older kids told them you had been shot. They were worried and are begging to come back home." In a much lower voice, he continued. "I overheard the two of them talking. Since their father died from a gunshot…"

I finished his sentence. "They're afraid I'm going to die too." My chest tightened.

"Exactly."

"Are they with you in your office right now?"

"Yes, they are," he said. "I'll put them on."

I heard muffled voices, then Matthew came on the line.

"Mom? Is it true you were shot?" The fear in his voice caused a lump in my throat.

"Yes, but I'm back from the hospital and getting stronger every day."

"Are you at home alone?"

"I'm staying with Mr. Danny and Miz Rachel, so I'm not alone. Don't worry. Everything is fine."

"Can we come home?"

"There are only a few days left before the camp session ends. Then you can come home. I promise you I'm going to be fine. Let me talk to your sister. I love you."

He mumbled something that sounded like "love you too." I had to smile.

Then Caroline spoke. "Are you hurting bad?"

"Only a little bit. I'm more tired than hurting. Miz Rachel is taking good care of me. Like I told Matthew, there's only a few days left before camp ends. Then you two can come home. I know you're worried about me because you can't see me in person, but I'm fine. I love you both very much."

I ended the call and sat quietly with the director's words echoing in my head. They lost their father to gunfire. They must be terrified they could also lose their mother. I should have made arrangements for them to come home. I phoned Tom Carlson back and told him I had changed my mind about the twins staying at camp.

"I can have one of the counselors drive them back to your home," he said.

"I hope that's not an inconvenience."

"Not at all," he said. "There are other children attending this session who have lost one of their police officer parents in the line of duty. We're especially tuned in to them."

I heaved a sigh of relief. "Thank you so much."

I went in search of Rachel to inform her of the latest developments. With the twins here, the situation would be much more chaotic, especially with Danny working on Melanie's case, not to mention Rachel and I delving into the other Haydel family murders. We needed to discuss the status quo.

I found her on the patio watering the arrangement of potted plants displayed there. She looked in my direction as I slid the glass door open.

"There's been a new development," I said, standing in the doorway.

"Oh?" She set the watering can down atop a white wrought iron table and walked toward me. Ushering me back inside she said, "You look upset. Has something happened to the twins?"

"In a way." I took a deep breath. "They're not physically hurt."

"They found out you were shot," she said.

I squeezed my eyes shut. "Yes, I didn't think they would."

"Come over here and sit." Rachel pulled a chair out from the kitchen table. "What happened?"

"The camp director phoned me. He said one of the older kids told them I'd been shot. The twins were overheard speaking to each other. They were afraid of losing me, since Jim died as a result of a gunshot wound."

Rachel shook her head. "Poor babies. They thought you might also die. Did you speak to them?"

"I did and tried to convince them otherwise. They wanted to come home, but I told them since there were only a few days left in the session, they should stay." I rubbed my face with both hands. "I couldn't forget how scared they both sounded. I called back and gave permission for them to come home. A counselor will be driving them back here soon."

"Good, they need to see you in person and be close to you. You made the right decision."

"With two extra people here, the best option for everyone is for me to move back over to my house."

She frowned. "Are you sure you're ready?"

"We live close enough that if I need anything or something happens, you, Danny, Josh, or even Remi can be there in a few seconds."

Rachel's expression changed at the mention of Remi's name. At that moment, I realized days had passed since Rachel said she had phoned.

"Speaking of Remi," I said, "why hasn't she been by here? She never called me back. Have you heard from her?"

"Remi was preparing to go on an assignment when she called me," Rachel began. "Nothing to do with Melanie's murder or the Haydel family." She paused for a long moment. "An unknown male attacked her on the street. Her photographer was still getting his gear out of the car and wasn't right behind her. He managed to get to her before something serious happened, but her attacker got away."

"She's not hurt, is she?" My heart skipped a beat.

"Minor injuries," she said. "She's been taking it easy at an undisclosed location."

I frowned. "She's in hiding? I can't see her doing that unless her attack is connected to Tracy's kidnapping and my shooting. You're not telling me the whole story."

"The man who attacked her threatened her for doing her interview with Tracy and also the one with Danny."

I felt heat rise to my face. "I know that man George Wilson who saw us together had something to do with everything that's happened. First Tracy, then me, and now Remi."

Thirty-five

Needless to say, the news about Remi disturbed me. I felt drained by the questions whirling around in my head. Did Rachel tell me Remi had only minor injuries so I wouldn't worry? Where could they be holding Tracy? Could she still be alive? Why can't this ordeal be over?

Rachel hovered around me, trying to calm me by asking if I wanted food or drink, but it made me more anxious. "Please stop. I need to get myself together before the twins arrive." I hated the hurt look on her face. "I'm sorry. This is all so exasperating and frightening."

She gave me a gentle hug. "Hopefully this will be over soon."

"The end can't come soon enough for me. God must be sending signs telling me to quit sticking my nose into every crime coming my way. You'd think I would have enough sense to listen."

"You didn't knowingly go into a dangerous situation when you went to the cemetery to visit Jim," Rachel said. "How were you to know Tracy would show up there? I wanted to dig into this case as much as you did. Stop beating yourself up."

A vehicle pulling up in the driveway caught my attention. I stood and walked over to the door. Rachel followed behind me.

My breath caught in my throat when the twins ran up to me. I wanted to hold on to them and never let them go.

"Mom," a breathless Matthew said. "You're squeezing me too tight."

I reluctantly released them from my embrace. "I'm so glad to see you."

"Matthew, Caroline," Rachel said, "come inside and get out of the heat. I have cold drinks and snacks for you."

Caroline gave me a cautious look. "Are you coming inside with us?"

"Of course," I assured her. "I want to speak to the counselor first."

After they followed Rachel inside, I greeted the woman who had been standing a short distance away. She introduced herself as Doctor Eve Raymond and explained to me her connection to law enforcement and the kids' camp.

"I'm a psychiatrist," she said. "I work with three police departments in the area. Normally I have sessions with officers who have killed someone in the line of duty or other personal problems. But the treating the grief of the children and spouses of fallen officers is too often overlooked."

"I can't thank you enough for bringing Matthew and Caroline back home."

"You're welcome." Doctor Raymond eyed my arm sling. "How much longer before the sling comes off?"

"I have a doctor's appointment tomorrow. I'll know more then."

"Good luck." She handed me a business card. "I also have a limited private practice. If you need anything, either for the kids or for yourself, give me a call."

I might do that, I thought. "Thank you," I said instead and watched for a few moments as she drove away.

I spent the rest of the day enjoying the company of my children and didn't even think about murder cases until around seven that evening. Josh phoned and said he would be back in about an hour.

"The kids are back from camp early," I said.

"Did something happen?"

"They found out I'd been shot. They were afraid I might die, since their father died from a gunshot wound."

"Aw, man," he said. "Poor kids. I can see why they might come to the same conclusion."

"Did this trip prove worthwhile?"

"You bet. Jack kept a lot of notes and even recorded a conversation he had with the authorities at the time of the so-called hit and run."

"How exciting."

"It'll be show-and-tell time when I get there."

I smiled at his enthusiasm. I could hardly wait to see what he'd come up with. And to see him again.

After ending the call, I discovered Danny and Rachel entertaining the twins with a board game.

"You want to play?" Caroline asked.

"No, y'all go ahead. I'll sit here and watch." I turned to Danny. "Josh will be back here in about an hour. The trip to Jennings proved to be productive."

"Sounds good," he said. "We could use some help with all of this."

His "all of this" took in a lot of crimes. Kidnapping, murder, attempted murder, and who knew what other illegal activities might be involved, or how many people had contributed to this tangled mess.

A little after eight, I heard Josh's truck drive up. In a short time, we could have the answers but I felt certain there would also be many more questions.

Thirty-six

"Okay, ladies," Danny said. "You'll have to keep the game going while Josh and I take care of business."

I stood and turned toward the two men. I opened my mouth to speak, but before I could utter a word, Josh walked over and stood directly in front of me, leaned closer, and spoke in a low voice. Apparently, he figured I intended to object.

"Danny and I decided it would be best if he and I went over what I learned on my trip. After the kids go to bed and are out of earshot, we'll discuss everything with you and Rachel."

I agreed and decided the twins didn't need to hear about more murder and mayhem. They've been faced with enough of that for most of their lives.

He and Danny left the room and disappeared down the hallway.

"Are they going to talk about who shot you?" Matthew asked.

Rachel and I exchanged a glance. "Not that I know of," I said. "The information Josh recovered on his trip has to do with another case."

Caroline pushed her chair away from the table. "I'm tired of playing games. Are we going to sleep over here tonight?"

"I thought it would be better if we stayed here. It's late and there's a lot of items to move, including Katy's things. Tomorrow we can move our belongings back over to our house."

She clapped her hands. "Yay! I'll be glad to sleep in my own bed. I didn't like the camp cot. The mattress felt lumpy."

"Can we go over and get some of our clothes and stuff if we're going to sleep here?" Matthew asked.

"Excellent idea," I said. "All the clothes you wore at camp must be dirty."

"Then tonight we can take baths at our own house," Caroline said.

"I suppose you can." They were most likely tired of camp bathrooms.

"I can get our other guest room ready for y'all," Rachel said. "You'll have to share the room. But there are twin beds in there so you don't have to share a bed."

I eyed the twins cautiously. "Is that arrangement okay with y'all?"

Neither child replied for a long moment. Finally, Caroline broke the silence.

"Okay. I think we'll be fine."

Matthew grumbled his agreement. I could tell he didn't like the idea of sharing a bedroom with his sister.

"It's only for one night," I said. "You'll be okay until tomorrow."

With bed and bath arrangements resolved, I ushered the kids next door to our house. An hour and a half later, we were back at the Marchands' house and I had the kids settled in bed.

"Mom," Matthew said. "Is Mr. Josh going to move into our house with us?"

I should have expected the subject to come up, but his inquiry caught me off guard. I sat on the side of his bed and directed my question to both him and Caroline. "Would you be upset if he did?"

"Kind of," he said, glancing at his sister.

"Not really," she said.

"Why would you be upset if Josh and I were living together? Would it make any difference if he and I got married?"

"What about Dad?" Matthew asked. "Don't you still love him?"

I heaved a sigh. "I know this is difficult for either of you to understand. I'll try to explain. I will always love your father. He was a wonderful man and a great father, but he can't be with us any longer. I feel certain he would not want me to spend the rest of my life alone."

"You won't be alone," Caroline said. "You have us."

They are so innocent. "I meant without an adult partner or husband. Besides, not too far into the future, y'all will be adults and have lives of your own."

They considered my words for a while. I'm sure they didn't fully understand the concept of my needing an adult partner or that they would soon be adults. To them becoming an adult seemed like an eternity away.

Matthew frowned. "Would we have to obey Mr. Josh if he moves in with us or you marry him?"

"I would hope you would. Listen, none of this is happening tonight or tomorrow or even next week. We can discuss all of this when and if the time comes." I gave each one a kiss and a hug. "Sleep tight."

Why does being a single mom and a widow have to be so difficult?

Thirty-seven

Danny seemed pleased with the results of Josh's trip. Rachel and I exchanged a glance. I could tell she was as anxious as I to hear what he had found. Could the death of Anne LeBlanc now be ruled a murder instead of a hit-and-run accident?

Josh pulled a chair out from the table for me to sit. He opened his briefcase and removed one of those old black and white composition books. The notebook with its stained and tattered cover had seen better days. "The 'papers' Jack had Adele store in a safe deposit box were more than notes. He wrote dates in this notebook and jotted down conversations he overheard."

"Nothing like the written word," I said. "What's the story?"

"Spoken like a true novelist," Rachel said.

We all laughed.

"As you might have guessed," Josh continued, "Carl LeBlanc, Anne's husband, paid off everyone involved, including Jack."

"Your cousin must have had second thoughts about his involvement," I said.

"According to what he wrote in the notebook, he felt bad about accepting the money," Josh said. "He and all the others were sworn to secrecy under threats of death. I mean, who would he tell? He couldn't very well go to the sheriff since he was in on the deal."

I shook my head in disgust. "Did Carl LeBlanc cut the brake line himself?"

"Either he or one of his minions," Danny said.

"I gather he found out about Anne's affair with a man named Phillip," Rachel said. "She wrote about him in her journal."

"Definitely," Josh agreed. "He set the incident up to look like a hit and run that occurred on her way home from meeting up with this guy."

"So, a drunk driver who left the scene never existed?" My question being rhetorical, since I already knew the answer.

"Not that we could uncover from this info," Josh said, pointing to the notebook.

Sometimes real life seemed a lot worse than a work of fiction, although this scenario had been used a number of times in mystery novels. Who knows? I might use it myself in a novel sometime in the future.

"Will this notebook and other related items be enough evidence to change the official record?" Rachel asked. We both turned to Danny.

"It's very possible. The problem is everyone involved is either deceased or not capable of being put on trial."

I made a face. "Like Gun Hebert?"

"Yeah, he's in a nursing home and has dementia. However, the tape recording of one conversation involving all the participants may be enough for the DA to make a legal decision of some kind. He may simply have the coroner change the death to homicide and say case closed."

"I don't understand how the copy of the real receipt from the garage managed to show up in the accident file," I said.

"Jack had a buddy in the sheriff's office who, by the way, also received a payoff; he managed to sneak it into the file in hopes that someone would discover it even if it happened years later. Guess he also had second thoughts about being paid off," Josh added. He removed an envelope from his briefcase and laid it on the table.

I eyed him with curiosity. "What's in there?"

"Five hundred dollars cash. Jack's payoff to fake the mechanic's report and to keep quiet."

"These days that wouldn't be enough money to keep someone quiet," I noted.

"Maybe five hundred dollars plus the death threat would," Danny said.

"I suppose so." Even though I write about murders, I can't imagine killing anyone for any amount of money. Although if they threatened my kids, I'd have to think hard about it.

"We're going to meet with Ronnie tomorrow," Danny said. "Then we'll take the file over to the DA's office. Maybe we'll at last be able to get closure on one of these Haydel family cases." He looked off into space for a short moment. "I sure as hell would like to be able to convict the person who killed Melanie. But more than that, we need to find Tracy."

"Maybe when we find Tracy, her mother's murder will be solved at the same time," I said. *But I pray the murderer isn't Tracy.*

Thirty-eight

Thursday, July 24

The aroma of freshly brewed coffee greeted me when I awoke. I peeked in on the kids, who were still asleep, then continued toward the familiar smell. Heading down the hall toward the kitchen, I heard Danny speaking on his cell phone.

"Great work." His excited tone led me to believe he had gotten good news.

Rachel turned to me when I entered the room. "Coffee?"

"Of course. I have to get my shot of caffeine before I can think clearly." I prepared my coffee at the counter and stirred in sugar and creamer. "I heard Danny on his phone. He sounded excited."

Rachel carried her cup to the table and sat across from me. "I hope he has good news. He's very upset about not being able to locate Tracy. I pray she's okay. He'd never forgive himself if she's..."

"Don't go there," I scolded. "George Wilson needs to be checked out. I firmly believe he is connected in some way to her kidnapping and my shooting."

Rachel shot me a curious look. "Who?"

Before I could answer her, Danny joined us in the kitchen. "Susan, one day I'm going to learn to take your instincts seriously."

I frowned. "What?"

"About the license plate you wanted me to run," he said. "Ronnie's deputies have been tailing Brett Lassiter since the day we talked to him at the station."

"And?" I prompted.

"Last night Lassiter met with a man at Bayou Pierre Bar. Their conversation sounded and looked antagonistic. After the man left, they ran the plate on his car, a blue Toyota. It's registered to a…"

"Barbara Wilson," Rachel and I said at the same time.

He gave a faux sigh. "Why am I not surprised you two knew this?"

"I figured you weren't going to check out George Wilson's car so I asked Josh to do it," I explained. "Then Rachel remembered seeing him at the bakery. She recognized him from the photo I'd taken of him."

"At the time he happened to be in a conversation with a woman named Barbara and called her Sis," Rachel continued. "Susan went to the bakery, but Barbara had quit the day before."

"I spoke to a woman I know who works there." I relayed our conversation. "Barbara wasn't well liked, it seems. When she quit, she told everyone she would be leaving town. Going back home to Shreveport."

Danny looked doubtful. "If she did leave town, she must have taken the bus or flown from Baton Rouge to Shreveport. Otherwise, her car wouldn't still be here."

A thought occurred to me. "Could she be the woman who made those phone calls to Remi and me?"

"She very well could be." Danny did a double take. "How do you know that man's name is George Wilson?"

"Oh," I said. "I guess I never got around to telling either of you. I found out his name when I went to the bakery. Then came my shooting and Tracy's kidnapping. And you know the rest. Actually, I don't know if his last name is Wilson or not. Wilson could be Barbara's married name."

Rachel shook her head. "I started to ask about the man when you first mentioned his name. And the second time I realized who he was. Dummy me. I should have guessed with the last name Wilson."

"You're not a dummy," I assured her. "There's so much going on and too many people involved."

"The name George is more than I knew at this point," Danny said. "I'll check the name out to see if he has a record."

Rachel appeared thoughtful for a long moment. "I told you about Anne's lover, didn't I?"

"Yes."

"In the same entry she discovered a single ruby earring in bed with Carl. It didn't belong to her, but reminded her of the ruby curse. She said as a child she'd heard about the curse from the Wilson kids."

"That's interesting. There is a connection to the Haydel family. Oh no…" I tapped my forehead with my hand. "My doctor's appointment is this morning. I completely forgot."

"You're right," Rachel said. "But we've got time. The appointment isn't until ten-thirty."

I glanced down at my clothing. Shorts and a raggedy tee. "I need to change from these old things. Guess I dressed in old clothes to move all our stuff back home." Then it hit me. "Someone will need to watch the kids. I'm perfectly able to drive myself to the doctor's office."

Rachel appeared hesitant. "Are you sure?"

"Yes, I am. The doctor is probably going to give me the go-ahead anyway."

"I'm not really convinced of that this soon," she said. "But I suppose when the kids wake up to find you gone, I can convince them you're okay."

"Good, I'm glad we've settled that. I'm going to go clean up and change clothes." I hoped the twins would awaken before I left so I could explain why I had to leave the house. They might not believe Rachel was telling the truth.

As it turned out, they did wander into the kitchen as I started for the door. With my purse on my shoulder, I couldn't have escaped without explaining. Moms and women in general never leave the house without their purses.

"I will be back as soon as I can from the doctor's office."

"Why do you have to go to the doctor?" Caroline asked.

I could see fear in her eyes. Matthew fidgeted with his pajama shirt.

"Because after a person has surgery, the doctor wants to check them out to make sure everything is healing correctly." I gave each of them a hug. "I'll be back soon."

Danny caught up with me outside on the way to my car. "George doesn't have a record. I found the picture you sent me a while back and his driver's license photo. I am sending a deputy to locate him and keep an eye on him. We can't arrest him for talking to another man in a bar. By the way, his last name is Wilson."

"Unless he's gotten scared and is staying out of sight, he's probably at the Court House Café. I suspect that's his regular routine. Good luck with finding him. He's involved up to his eyeballs."

"I believe it."

"What about Brett Lassiter?"

He shrugged. "I'll continue to have him surveilled until I can find a legitimate reason to get a search warrant for his place."

"Do you think it's possible Brett Lassiter is behind Tracy's kidnapping and George Wilson is working for him?"

"I considered the possibility, but I can't figure out a motive for Lassiter to take her unless she did kill her mother and he's trying to get her out of the country."

Thirty-nine

The doctor gave me the okay to drive, but warned me not to go overboard. No heavy lifting or any other strenuous activities. He suggested I would benefit from a few sessions of physical therapy. However, due to the limited treatment available in our small parish, I would have to attend the sessions in New Orleans. The idea didn't appeal to me. I firmly declined, so he gave me a pamphlet with instructions for light exercises to strengthen my arm and shoulder.

Doctor Richard had been my primary care physician for years so I could tell by his tone of voice he had given me the okay against his better judgment.

I felt a little strange leaving Doctor Richard's office without the sling on my arm, but I would not have a problem getting back to some semblance of normalcy.

I got into my blazing hot car. *A little shade in the parking lot would have been nice.* Starting the engine, I turned on the air conditioner full blast.

My instincts told me George Wilson was heavily involved in my shooting. I couldn't identify the man who shot me because of his mask and the chaos of the situation, but it wouldn't surprise me if George were the shooter. Despite the heat still lingering in the car, I felt a chill. The terror I'd experienced at that moment came rushing back.

I couldn't help wondering about George's connection to Brett Lassiter. I decided to swing by the Court House Café just for the heck of it to see if George was following his usual routine of having his coffee and reading the newspaper as if he didn't have a care in the world.

I spotted the blue Toyota parked in front of the café and slowed my car. Should I go inside? Maybe it would be a better idea to go back home to my kids.

Curiosity got the better of me. I found a place to park where I had a clear view of the door. I glanced at my watch. A quarter past eleven. He was running a little late today. The other times I'd seen him leaving here much earlier, more like nine-thirty.

Sitting in the stuffy car without the motor running for more than fifteen minutes proved to be pretty uncomfortable. Sweat dripped down in between my breasts.

Just as I'd resigned myself to give up and go home, the subject of my surveillance walked out of the café. He had someone with him. A woman with the blackest hair I'd ever seen accompanied him down the sidewalk toward the Toyota. Could she be Barbara?

Not long after the pair started walking, a man emerged from the café and watched them for a few minutes. He wore jeans and a vee neck t-shirt, but I recognized him as a deputy named Logan Hahn. He must be the one tailing George Wilson. The surveillance had landed into much better hands than mine.

I left the parking space to head home. I had started feeling slightly woozy anyway. Probably just the heat.

Upon my arrival at the Marchands' house, both the kids and Rachel greeted me with excitement, but not for the same reason.

"Wow," Matthew said, "the doctor let you take off the arm sling. We're glad you're home."

"You took a long time," Caroline said. "I didn't think you were coming back."

I gave both kids a hug. Glancing at Rachel, I said, "I came back as soon as I could. I'm sorry I worried you." The mention of my detour wouldn't help ease their fears. I might not tell Rachel either.

"When we get a moment," she said in a soft voice, "there's news about the DNA on those cigarette butts Danny found at the cemetery."

"Good news, I hope."

"I sure hope so." She gave me a suspicious look. "You look like you could use a cold drink."

I swear she must be able to read my mind and could tell I looked hot because I had been sitting in a hot car for a while when I should have come straight back.

"I would love a glass of iced tea," I said.

"I hope you don't mind my raiding your freezer for those popsicles you had in there," she said. "I gave the twins each one."

"My goodness, I can't believe there were any left. I guess popsicles don't go bad."

The kids settled down to watch a children's program on a local PBS television station while Rachel and I sat at the kitchen table and sipped on iced tea.

"Is Danny at the station?" I asked.

"Of course. They got a DNA match on one of the cigarette butts." She took a swallow of her tea. "They took the man into the sheriff's office to be 'interviewed.'"

My heartbeat sped up. "A match! Who is he?"

"Danny wouldn't say. He simply told me the man had once been convicted of a felony, so that's how they have his DNA on file. He's on parole now."

Not George Wilson, for sure. "I hope he's part of the gang that shot me, kidnapped Tracy, and tried to attack Remi." I considered the odds, but didn't think they were in our favor. Afraid to have too much hope, I guess. "There doesn't seem to be a good chance of this guy's involvement."

Rachel frowned. "Why not?"

"Think about it," I said. "Convicted felons aren't always up to no good. He could work for the cemetery. Many businesses hire ex-cons to give them a second chance." I had a little bit of a soft spot in my heart for one particular ex-con named Gibb Romaine, who had saved my life almost three years ago.

Her smile seemed forced, but her tone of voice determined. "I refuse to be pessimistic. I say there is at least a sixty percent chance of him being one of the participants in the crime."

"I'll try to be positive. Although I don't know how you came up with a sixty percent chance."

Six days had passed since Tracy, Remi and I were attacked and there was still no word on Tracy's whereabouts. I had a hard time staying positive. Both Rachel and I seemed to find our emotions see-sawing up and down. Thinking positive one minute, and then losing hope the next.

"We could get a miracle. You never know."

"We could sure use one."

Forty

Danny's solemn expression indicated his interview with the suspect hadn't gone well. He plopped down onto a kitchen chair. "He lawyered up."

"Which probably means he's guilty." I tried not to sound disheartened by the news, and at the same time hopeful.

He frowned. "Guilty of something, but not necessarily any involvement in this case."

"I suppose he could've been dealing drugs in the cemetery." Rachel's voice sounded as disappointed as mine.

My curiosity went wild. "Who is this guy?"

"Jeff Boudreau. He's been arrested a few times for assault and illegal use of a weapon."

My heart skipped a beat. *Could he be the one who shot me?*

Danny pounded his fist on the table. "It's so damn frustrating. If I knew for sure he was selling drugs when he left those cigarette butts there, I could hold him on parole violations plus intent to distribute. Then we'd have time to find evidence if he's involved with the murder."

I eyed him with caution. "Is anything going on with Brett Lassiter?"

"Nothing much. He's been keeping a low profile since we had our talk at the station."

"You'd think he would be trying to contact you or Ronnie about whether there's been any word on his daughter's kidnapping," Rachel said.

"Any normal father would be pestering the hell out of the police or at least going to the media for help in finding her."

"Maybe he has considered going to the media," I suggested. "There have been a number of cases in other parts of the country where a family member, usually a wife, goes missing and the husband goes to a local TV station. He acts worried and scared when all the time he's the guilty party."

"I'm not sure if he would even consider giving a press conference. Those guys always believe they're smarter than us. But I have a problem reading Lassiter. At the time of Melanie's murder, he cooperated to a certain extent, but was not entirely accommodating."

"What do you mean?" I asked.

"When we asked him to come in for another interview, he would agree to a certain day, but when the time came, he was suddenly unavailable."

"The deputies who are keeping tabs on him don't see anything odd or out of place at his house?" Rachel asked.

I frowned. "I thought about the same thing myself. He's simply staying in his home and not going anywhere?"

"Lassiter hasn't left the apartment, but every couple of hours a different man leaves and drives off. According to the deputies, he'll return a few hours later. There are four vehicles associated with these men."

"How weird is that? Where are they going?"

"That's a good question. We don't have any deputies available to tail these guys. I might see if Josh can do some work for me."

"I'm sure he'll be happy to." I don't know what made me think of my next question. "This is probably a silly question. What are they doing for food? Delivery? Take-out?"

"That's about it," he said. "There's been a lot of pizza and other fast food being delivered. I'm beginning to wonder if Lassiter is even in there. He could be holed up somewhere else." He appeared to consider an idea, then stood and left the room, keying in a number on his phone.

"Don't you find that whole scene odd?"

Rachel's expression clouded. "Indeed, I do. I think Danny may have had an epiphany."

"And he's about to put a plan in place."

Danny appeared pleased when he returned to the kitchen. "We're going to find out who's staying in that apartment. I should've thought of this before. Or at least, should have remembered how sneaky Lassiter is."

I perked up. "What are y'all going to do?"

He smiled. "Let's just say we're going into the food delivery business."

"I hope your plan works," I said.

"Keep your fingers crossed. Now I have some other business to wrap up." His jaw muscles tensed. "Ronnie and I have an appointment with DA Blanchard to show him what we have on Anne LeBlanc's murder. I sure hope Blanchard thinks we have enough for the grand jury to hear the case."

"He should," Rachel said. "The conversation on the tape tells the whole story."

Danny lifted his hands, palms up. "*Should* and *would* are two different things. You know how these things go. Blanchard's a stickler about every little detail. This case is different from any others he's tried; you can't count on him agreeing. Also, since there's no defendant to prosecute and the incident happened so long ago, he may not want to stir up a hornet's nest."

After he left, Rachel and I sat for a while in silence. Everything in Louisiana involves politics. For all I knew, the DA had some higher political aspirations and would not want to ruffle the feathers of an important backer. I could only hope otherwise.

Finally, I decided to get started bringing all our clothes and other belongings back to our own house. They weren't going to move themselves.

~ * ~

"Someone has been tailing me," George said. "I think the cops saw me talking to Brett Lassiter at the bar."

"Why would they be following you?" she asked.

"Don't be naïve, Barbara. They suspect Lassiter of something and believe I'm involved with him."

"Well, you are. You should be more careful."

George let his irritation fade. He had grown tired of this seemingly futile endeavor of finding the ruby. "I think it's time for us to leave town." *Or for me to give myself up.*

"No way," she shouted. "We're not leaving until we get our hands on the ruby. Lassiter can lead us to it."

Forty-one

I felt exhausted after moving the kids' and my things back to our house. Hard to believe such little activity would be so tiring. There weren't a lot of items to move, plus I had help. Still, my shoulder ached slightly. Permission to discard the arm sling may have been given prematurely. I thought about climbing into bed and disappearing under the covers.

Tracy continued to haunt my thoughts. I prayed they hadn't killed her. Other questions about her whole family lingered in my mind. Could she have killed her mother? What triggered the idea that she had been the killer? Her exact words had been, "The killer *might* be me."

Harriet Haydel's journal called to me. I wanted to delve deeper into what her state of mind had been since the day Mya gave birth to Charles' illegitimate son. Could she have pushed her husband over the balcony to his death? Hardly the act of the daughter of two Christian missionaries.

My cell phone rang and interrupted my contemplations. Josh's number appeared on the display. I wondered why I hadn't heard from him in a while.

"How's everything going?" he asked in a low voice. "Sorry I couldn't help with the move back to your place."

"Don't worry about that. I had plenty of help. I also made sure the kids did their share."

"Are they okay?" I detected a hint of concern in his voice.

"They are almost back to normal...almost." I gave a soft laugh. "They were upset when I had to leave for my doctor's appointment, but when I came back, they relaxed a little."

"What did the doctor say?"

"He gave me permission to drive and said I don't have to wear the arm sling. He warned me not to go overboard with activity."

"Good advice."

"I don't think I'll be doing a whole lot for a while. I still feel tired. By the way, what have you been up to?"

"Danny has me doing some tail and stake out work."

"Oh, yeah. He mentioned 'hiring' you to follow those men."

"That's about it. Another man just drove up. I'll talk to you later."

"Be careful."

He said he would and ended the call.

Those men were guarding something or someone in that house. Tracy? The ruby? Or both? Not likely the ruby would be there, unless the men didn't know what they were guarding. I doubted Brett Lassiter would trust any of them being alone with such a valuable gem. I wouldn't.

A twinge of apprehension about Josh's safety pierced my chest. I shook off the feeling. If I was going to continue getting involved with men who serve in some law enforcement capacity, I needed to learn to deal with the anxiety. Believe me, it wasn't easy. I simply had to keep in mind that Josh is quite capable of dealing with any situation that might come up. Anyone who can do policing in a war zone knows how to handle the worst.

Back to Harriet's journal. Flipping through the pages, a name in the entry dated March 30, 1930, caught my eye.

We had a small wedding ceremony for Chun and Thomas Wilson, our gardener. I conducted a ceremonial Burmese rite, which I had seen many times while living in Burma. I joined the palms of the couple and wrapped them in white cloth. Their joined palms were then dipped into perfumed water in a silver bowl. The Burmese word for "to marry" literally means "to join palms together." Of course, I also prayed over them in my Christian tradition. They didn't have much choice in the matter because of Louisiana's ban against mixed marriages. Although the law basically prevented Blacks and Whites from marrying, the clerk had decided the law referred to Asians as well. He refused to issue a marriage license. I felt God blessed their union during this ceremony.

Chun looked lovely in the ankle-length pink satin dress which she had brought from her home in Rangoon years ago. Pink flowers adorned her dark hair. Surprisingly, Thomas agreed to wear a pink taipon, a traditional Burmese shirt and long gray longyi or pants. Even the boy dressed in pink longyi, which imitated those worn by adult men.

I've finally managed to stop regarding him as a symbol of Charles' betrayal. The child was not at fault. I have prayed daily to ask God to give me the strength to discontinue blaming him for Charles' sin. His name is Lin, which means bright. And he is indeed a bright little boy.

Thomas Wilson? So that was the Wilson-Haydel connection. How fascinating. I knew all along that George and Barbara Wilson had a connection to the family. This information confirmed my belief. I still wanted to know more.

~ * ~

Josh zoomed in with his camera to get a close-up of the newcomer's face. He figured that the other man would soon leave the house. The men seemed to be on four-hour shifts. Whoever they were guarding must not be a big flight risk. He doubted Lassiter would trust anyone other than himself if the object were of high value, like the ruby. The old saying about no honor among thieves came to mind. They had to be guarding a person. Tracy perhaps?

Minutes passed and the first man had not walked out the door. Josh scanned the house with his binoculars. He noticed what seemed like movement behind the curtains in a window on the side of the house. Hoping to see more, he set his gaze on that spot. No such luck. No movement. For the time being, he blew off any suspicions. An A/C or a fan could have stirred them.

His truck was in a perfect spot, hidden from view of the house, but in the right place for him to be able to see comings and goings. The only problem was the heat. It was hell to be on a stake-out during the summer in Louisiana. Wiping sweat from his forehead, he continued his watch.

Finally, a man exited the back door and left in his vehicle, an old model Dodge Ram pickup. Josh checked his watch and jotted the departure time in his notebook.

The curtains moved once more. An almost imperceptible figure emerged but quickly disappeared behind the hangings. Was someone trying to figure out an escape route?

He needed to get closer to the house on foot, but not in broad daylight. It would be a few more hours until dark.

Then he saw her. She appeared to be attempting to open the window. In a flash she disappeared from view.

Josh keyed in Danny's cell number. "This is where Tracy is being held. I saw her in the window. I believe she might be trying to figure out a way to escape. I could give her a hand."

"Stay put," Danny said in a stern voice. "There will be backup. We got a visit from George Wilson. He's talking about everything, going all the way back to Melanie's murder. My deputies watching Lassiter's apartment informed me Lassiter is on the move with another man. I have a deputy tailing them. They're most likely on the way to your location. In which case, Ronnie and I will be joining y'all at the scene along with SWAT."

Forty-two

The sound of an approaching vehicle grabbed Josh's attention. He expected to see the truck carrying Lassiter and one of his men.

Instead, the Dodge Ram pickup driven by the man who had recently left came roaring back into the driveway. Its driver appeared to reach for something on the passenger seat and then opened his door, attempting to exit.

Before he could get out, a blue Toyota, followed by a battered red pickup, hemmed the driver in. Two men and a woman jumped out of the Toyota and two more men exited the red pickup. They all carried guns.

What the hell is going on here? Josh snapped close-ups of the group with his camera. Putting the camera down, he reached in the truck console for his gun and placed it on the passenger seat. That group sure wasn't law enforcement, he thought. He'd bet his last dollar the Toyota was the car Susan had asked him to trace. That woman could be Barbara Wilson, the vehicle owner.

Josh continued to watch as the group marched the Ram pickup driver into the house at gunpoint. He keyed in Danny's cell number. "Something crazy going on here."

"What?"

"Four guys and a woman got out of two different vehicles and ushered one of the men doing guard duty here into the house at gunpoint."

"Not what I wanted to hear. Lassiter and his man are almost to your location. When they see those other vehicles, they might not stop. We're on our way. Don't try to get any closer to the situation. I don't want you to get hurt. You're not law enforcement. Understood?"

"Understood." Josh agreed, but didn't like not being in on the action. He'd give anything to come face to face with the scumbag who'd shot Susan.

A few minutes later, a white pickup came to a stop about twenty feet away from the house. A brown Chevy Malibu slowed some distance behind the pickup.

All at once, sirens filled the air. Josh glanced around the area to determine the location of the officers. He spotted two units with lights flashing come around a curve and stop in front of the white pickup. The Malibu driver closed in behind the pickup to block any chance of escape.

All hell is about to break loose. Josh grabbed his camera and started recording a video as the officers surrounded the vehicle. He recognized Ronnie Hart and heard him order the occupants out of the truck.

Josh had used his camera on a number of occasions while working different cases, but this almost felt like documenting a news story. An interesting thought. A new career as a TV news photographer?

After a long pause, the driver side door opened and a man stepped out with his hands in the air. Seconds later, the passenger did the same. The two men were taken into custody.

An armored vehicle arrived and men in SWAT gear exited, slowly heading toward the front door of the house in single file.

Danny addressed the occupants of the house over a speaker. "We have you surrounded. Release Tracy Lassiter. Let her go."

The door to the house remained closed. Danny repeated his commands.

In case those guys came out shooting, Josh laid a hand on his gun, more from reflex than need. He shook his head and removed his hand, then returned to his camera to continue videoing the scene. Even if they did come out shooting, he wouldn't be involved in returning fire. There were enough officers out there to take care of the situation.

He hoped those dirtbags would give up peacefully. His own shooting of Keith Parker last year still came back to haunt him periodically. At least Parker hadn't died. Josh glanced at the scar on his arm. Shrapnel from his tour in Iraq. He shook off his reflections.

After what seemed like a long time, the front door opened slowly and a shaky Tracy Lassiter stepped out. A SWAT officer rushed over and pulled her away to safety.

"People in the house, come out with your hands up," Danny ordered. "One at a time."

No one emerged. The SWAT team rushed into the house, shouting commands and more than a few expletives.

Shortly, handcuffed men and the lone woman were escorted out and placed in patrol cars to be taken to jail. Josh watched with satisfaction. No shots fired. Nobody got hurt.

Whatever evidence this guy George Wilson had given Danny must have been a gold mine.

Forty-three

Danny peered through the one-way window of the interrogation room. Lassiter fidgeted in the chair. *Good. He's nervous.*

Lassiter turned his head when Danny entered the room. "Why in hell did you haul me and my men in here? We were going to rescue my daughter. That Wilson bunch had her kidnapped and were holding her there."

"Really," Danny said. "Our evidence doesn't support your statement."

Lassiter shot him an angry look. "What evidence?"

Danny answered his question with another question. "What were two of your men doing in that house before you arrived?"

He folded his arms. "They weren't my men."

"Then why were they seen going in and out of your apartment numerous times before ending up there? A witness stated he saw them come and go at that house about every four hours or so."

Lassiter frowned. He clasped and unclasped his hands several times.

"After you were informed of Tracy's kidnapping, you never asked us about the status. You never went to the media to ask for her safe return, like any good father would." Danny kept his gaze steady on the suspect's face. No reaction.

Then Lassiter broke eye contact with Danny and looked down at the table. "I was trying to protect her."

"Protect her from what?"

"From herself. She killed her mother, although she claims not to remember."

"Do you think if she were hypnotized, she might recall the incident?"

Lassiter didn't speak for a long moment. "It's possible, but that's not allowed in court, is it?"

"You're right. In that respect, hypnosis is similar to polygraph tests. They're basically tools to help us find the truth. But we now have evidence to support a different killer, not Tracy. And this evidence *can* be presented in court."

"Like who?"

"I'm looking at him," Danny said. "And I have a recorded conversation to prove it."

"This interview is finished. I want an attorney."

"You're going to need a good one."

Lassiter leaned back in the chair. "What am I being charged with?"

"The murder of Melanie LeBlanc and the arranging of the kidnapping of your daughter, Tracy. When I find out which one of your men was responsible for shooting Susan Foret, he's going to be charged with attempted murder."

"I told him no—" Lassiter clamped his mouth shut.

Danny walked to the door and stepped out. He motioned for a deputy to take Lassiter to jail. In the hallway he spotted Ronnie, who motioned him into his office.

"I questioned a member of the Wilson group named Joel Chin. According to him, he and his cousin Russell Wilson were in the cemetery the day of Tracy's kidnapping. They had planned to grab Susan."

Danny raised an eyebrow. "Susan?"

"To keep her from investigating," Ronnie explained. "Then Tracy showed up, followed by Lassiter's men. They hid in some bushes and saw the whole thing go down."

"George Wilson indicated his family kept going against his orders to lay low. Barbara made threatening phone calls to Susan and Remi," Danny said. "But he did admit to ordering his nephew Russell to get rid of Tracy. He thought the kid had more sense than to shoot at her in front of a police station."

"Wilson's been charged with arranging the shooting of you and Tracy. His nephew Russell will be charged with the actual shooting. But I'm asking the DA to come up with a plea deal for George because of his cooperation with us," Ronnie said. "Is that good with you?"

"Yeah, I would agree to that, provided he agrees to testify in court against everyone, including his family members. That tape recording of the conversation between him and Lassiter is invaluable. It wraps up my murder case in a nice neat bundle."

Ronnie smiled. "The murder case of Melanie LeBlanc is closed."

"There is one other thing I'd like to do," Danny said. "If Tracy is willing to be hypnotized, I want to have her go under."

"But we can't use anything she says under hypnosis in court. What if it turns out she and Lassiter worked together on the murder?"

"I'll think about that when and if it happens. I firmly believe she witnessed her father murder her mother and was so traumatized she blocked the memory of it out of her mind. Lassiter probably kept telling her that she killed her mother so she started to believe she did."

"In other words, this would be for Tracy's benefit. So she wouldn't have any doubts."

"Exactly."

Forty-four

Josh called me with the good news. "Tracy's been rescued."

I heaved a sigh of relief; my eyes teared up. "Thank God. They must have been holding her at that house. Where is she now?"

"I have no idea, but she is safe."

Not if she killed her mother. She'll be sent to jail. "What else happened?"

"Lassiter and his men, along with Barbara Wilson and other family members of hers, were taken into custody at the house where I did my stakeout. I don't know any other specifics, so until Danny or Ronnie announces charges or other details, it's best not to spread the news around."

"I won't say anything except to Rachel. Do you know if they arrested George Wilson there?"

"Not at this place," he said. "Danny indicated to me that Wilson turned himself in and gave them a load of evidence."

My heart did a flip. "What a surprise!"

"No kidding," he said. "I'm going to drop by the sheriff's office and leave them my tapes. I got the whole event on video. At least everything that happened outside."

"Will you come by here later?"

"Of course," he said. "I need to clean up and rest a little. Believe it or not, sitting in a hot car for hours on end is tiring."

I understood perfectly.

For a long moment after we ended our call, I sat thinking over the limited information he had given me. But from the sound of it, Danny may have Melanie's murder case wrapped up, with Brett Lassiter as her killer and not Tracy. *Hopefully I'm not guilty of wishful thinking about Tracy. The only cold case left to solve now is the death of Charles Haydel.*

There were a few pages remaining in Harriet's journal I needed to read. My two unanswered questions could very well be in her writings. Did she push her husband off the balcony? What happened to the ruby?

Cries of "Mom, we're hungry" postponed my search through the last pages of Harriet's journal. After I prepared the twins a snack, I returned to my security blanket chair, intent on reading those pages.

Then another brief interruption. Rachel knocked on the door. I waved for her to come inside and sit in the den with me.

"I have news," she said.

"About Tracy?" I hated to spoil any surprise she had intended. "I know."

She made a face. "Josh, I presume."

"Of course."

"I also have news about Remi," she said.

"Oh, is she all right?"

"Yes, she's coming out of hiding and headed to our house. Danny called and gave me that bit of news, and he firmly believes they have their murder case complete, with Brett Lassiter as Melanie LeBlanc's killer."

"Josh mentioned something about George Wilson. Danny told him the man turned himself in and gave them the evidence they needed to file charges against Melanie's killer." I raised my index finger in the air. "That reminds me. I found a small connection between the Haydel family and the Wilsons."

Rachel perked up. "Really?"

I told her about the wedding between Chun, the Burmese nanny, and a Thomas Wilson. "I'd like to go further down the line to see where George and Barbara Wilson fit in."

A vehicle pulling into the Marchands' driveway caught my attention. Dizziness almost overcame me as I turned to view the car.

"Remi's here!" Rachel jumped up; her voice held a combination of excitement and relief.

She didn't seem to notice my sudden distress. I took deep breaths and followed Rachel out the door.

"Welcome back to the world," I joked and hugged Remi. "Seriously, I'm so glad you're safe."

Remi's eyes teared. "That goes both ways, girl. Good to see you up and around."

"Let's go inside my house," I said, with a voice as shaky as my trembling legs.

"Susan, are you alright?" Remi put her arm on my shoulder.

"No, she's not." Rachel ushered me inside and ordered me to sit in my chair. "What's wrong? You look pale."

"I felt dizzy before I went outside. I thought the problem had passed, but it came back worse." My vision dimmed. I vaguely heard Rachel's voice. "Call nine-one-one, Remi."

I tried to object, but my world went dark.

~ * ~

The television on without audio glowed and served as a nightlight in the dark room. For a few minutes I couldn't remember what had happened. My shoulder ached and I felt groggy. Oh, yes. I passed out. What in the world happened? I must be in the hospital again. Where was everybody?

The door to my room opened. I squinted in the glare from the hall light. A female figure entered. A nurse, maybe. To my relief, the woman turned out to be Remi.

"You're awake," she said softly.

"Barely," I whispered. "What happened?"

"After you passed out, EMS brought you here. The doctors discovered you were bleeding internally from your wound. Steven donated blood for you."

My sweet brother. "Is he here?"

"Yes, I'll trade places with him. You're in ICU, so only one visitor at a time." She left the room and soon Steven appeared at my bedside.

"Hey, Susie. As usual, you gave us all a scare." He smiled, so at least he wasn't angry with me.

"I should have stayed longer at the hospital the first time or else not talked the doctor into letting me get rid of the arm sling."

"Maybe you shouldn't have tried to move back into your own house so soon. You know Rachel didn't mind taking care of you at all."

I sighed. "I thought having the twins there would be too much commotion."

He clasped my hand. "Don't worry about the kids. Megan and I are always available to take care of them. In fact, I'm going to relieve Rachel, so she can come up here."

"Thanks for donating your blood," I said.

"No problem. Glad to do it. If you hadn't made it…"

"Don't think about that. I'll be fine. Does Josh know?"

"Yeah, he should be up here any time now. You need anything?"

"I need some pain medication for my shoulder. Where's the call button for the nurse?"

He checked the side of the bed, pulled out the remote and pressed the correct button. I told the nurse what I needed. She said she'd be right in.

"Steven, do Mother and Dad know I'm back in the hospital?"

"I spoke to Dad. Expect to see them both up here soon."

"What I expect will be more scolding from Mother," I said.

"Think positively. Maybe she won't get on you because she'll be so glad you're going to be okay."

"Dreamer."

The nurse arrived and administered the pain medicine through my IV. I said goodbye to Steven as I drifted off to sleep.

Visions filled with snapshots of a gun pointed at me and a fierce blow to my shoulder swirled around during my drug-induced sleep. Would I ever be back to normal?

Forty-five

Friday, July 25

I awoke occasionally throughout the night. Josh dozed in a chair one of those times. Then Rachel appeared in that spot another time. I didn't realize until morning that I'd received special treatment. Normally patients in ICU were only allowed visitors, one at a time, until the end of visiting hours. Then the hospital rules allowed one relative to spend the night in the room. Exceptions were made, because Rachel and Josh were not blood relatives.

My special treatment didn't extend to Doctor Theriot. He strode into my room looking stern. His dark eyes, like Danny's blue ones, let you know when he wasn't happy with you for not following his instructions.

Retaining a doctor who displayed anger at your decisions may seem strange to a lot of people, but Doctor Theriot had taken care of Jim that fateful day. He and the other doctors treated him with dignity, even though like most people at the time, they thought he had committed suicide.

"I'm not happy to see you making a return visit to the hospital," the doctor said. "This time, young lady, you are not going to talk me into allowing you to leave before I think you're ready."

I lowered my eyes. "Understood." I felt too weak to argue anyway.

"Now, let's get your vitals."

He finished taking my blood pressure and remarked, "Blood pressure is not great, but better than I expected."

I asked him, point-blank, "What caused the bleeding?"

"A blood vessel had been nicked by the bullet. Unfortunately, the surgeon missed the cut because of muscle tissue swelling in the area. It didn't take long for the bleeding to begin in earnest after the swelling went down and your activity level went up."

"In other words, if I had stayed in the hospital longer or kept the sling on longer, the bleeding might have been contained before I ended up back in the hospital."

"In my opinion, yes to the former. If you had stayed in the hospital longer, we would have discovered the problem here before it became a problem for you at home. The bleeding would have been caught through blood work or simply through taking your vitals." He studied me with his dark-eyed gaze. "How were you feeling prior to passing out?"

"For several days before, I felt very tired, but I thought that might be normal for someone who had recently undergone surgery."

"Fatigue can be a side effect from surgery, but not to the point of fainting. The problem has been corrected and it's up to you to follow my directions until you are completely healed."

He finished his exam and turned to leave. I came close to asking him for an approximate date of discharge.

He must have read my mind. Turning back to face me, he said, "You'll be in ICU for one more night and then tomorrow you'll be moved to a regular room. After that, we'll take it one day at a time. Take it easy and get as much rest as you can."

How is that possible here, or even at my house?

Shortly after Doctor Theriot left, Rachel came in. "I assume from the look on the doctor's face and on yours, either he gave you a hard time for trying to do too much too soon, or your exam didn't go well."

"The former," I admitted. "But I don't believe fault in this situation falls entirely on me. If I normally spent time suing people, I would file suit."

She frowned. "Why?"

"I know some of this situation is my fault, but damage to a blood vessel created by the bullet went unnoticed during the original surgery."

"Why didn't they catch it?"

"Supposedly muscle swelling concealed this other damage, so they missed it."

A frown creased her brow. "That's not like these doctors or this hospital. However, doctors are human. They make mistakes. You're going to recover if you follow doctor's orders this time."

"Exactly what he said."

"I hope you're not truly considering suing anyone," she said.

"No, I guess not. Just trying to absolve myself of guilt. You know how I am about following orders. Besides, I more or less told Doctor Theriot the last time that I would check myself out of the hospital if he didn't release me.

"I'm not a good example for my kids," I continued. "They'll think it's okay to disobey orders. On a number of occasions, Matthew has acted like following orders wastes his time."

Rachel shook her head. "They'll be fine." She removed her cell phone from her purse. "Speaking of the twins, they asked if you would do a virtual visit with them, so they would know you were still alive."

I grimaced. "Did they actually say they wanted to make sure I hadn't died?"

"Yes, they did."

~ * ~

Tracy's legs trembled as she walked into the psychiatrist's office. She glanced back at Danny, who gave her an encouraging smile.

Her loss of memory about certain parts of the event made her question everything she had told herself for years. For this reason, yesterday she'd contacted Megan, Susan's sister-in-law, to represent her at the hypnosis session.

Her heart beat so fast and hard, she thought Danny might be able to hear it. *Where's Megan? She wouldn't desert me.* How would Danny react when the attorney arrived? She hadn't informed him of her agreement with Megan.

My father is in jail today, charged with my mother's murder, but I can't be certain whether he only confessed to save me from going to prison or if he's guilty. Although Danny did mention something about a tape recording on which her father had been caught making arrangements for the murder. Still, she feared she might somehow be connected to the crime. But why would her father have her kidnapped? One of his men even shot Susan.

She took a seat in the small waiting room. Danny sat in the chair next to her.

"Try to relax," he said in a soft voice. "You don't have anything to worry about."

"How can you be so sure I have nothing to fear?"

"I've been in law enforcement for pretty close to thirty years," he said. "Most of that time I've been able to read people well enough to know whether they're guilty or not." He gave a slight shrug. "I don't have a one hundred percent record, but more like ninety-eight percent."

She sat on the edge of the seat and gripped the arms of the chair with her hands. "I'm still afraid that the truth will be bad for me. Like I might have killed her."

"I'm confident that's not the case." He smiled. "Relax. That's an order."

"Okay, I'll try." She took a deep breath and leaned back in the chair. She needed to tell him about Megan. "Danny, I asked..."

A door leading to the doctor's private office opened and interrupted her confession. A tall woman with shoulder-length dark hair appeared in the doorway. Tracy's heartbeat sped up.

The woman gave a pleasant smile and beckoned them to enter. "I'm Doctor Alicia Bordelon. You must be Tracy," she said, extending a hand to her.

Tracy shook her hand. Looking around, she stopped before entering the room. "Wait. I hope you don't mind, but I asked Megan to be here. I'm sure she'll be here any moment now."

Danny frowned. "Megan? Did you really believe you needed a lawyer?" His words carried a hint of frustration.

"I wanted to be prepared in case. I'm sorry to spring this on you. You've been nothing but kind to me during this whole ordeal."

"Why don't you two come on into my office and relax until she arrives," Doctor Bordelon suggested. "Tracy, I need to get some information about you before we start the procedure."

"Are you sure a third person in the room isn't going to cause a problem?" Danny asked, looking concerned. "I requested the hypnotism session, not in connection with the official homicide case. As far as I'm concerned, the murderer is in jail. I simply wanted to put Tracy's mind at ease."

"Don't worry, Danny. You and Megan will be out of Tracy's view. That shouldn't be a problem. Tracy, if having both of them in here will make you feel more relaxed, then it's good."

Megan rushed into the office carrying her briefcase. "I'm sorry I'm late. A last-minute phone call delayed me." She turned her attention to Danny. "I overheard your last remark. If that's the case, I, as her attorney, should be in the room instead of you, a police officer."

Danny clenched his jaw. He glanced from Megan to Tracy, and then to the doctor. "Tracy?"

"I would prefer to have only Megan accompany me," she said. "I'm sorry, Danny. It's nothing personal. In case you're wrong about my innocence, I'll need legal protection."

"If that's the way you want to do this, it's your decision," he said. "Keep in mind that what you reveal under hypnosis is not allowed in court."

"I know," Tracy said. "Megan informed me of that point when I contacted her. If I admit to killing my mother, I know you would not let me get away with murder. You're too dedicated an officer. I told Megan in our phone conversation that if I confessed to murder under hypnosis, I would turn myself in to the police."

Forty-six

Danny leaned forward in his chair, watching Megan and Tracy enter the psychiatrist's office. Could he have been wrong in his belief of Tracy's innocence? She sure seemed determined to believe in her culpability. Could it be possible her missing memories about the event had already come back to her? Of course it was. But until now, he had dismissed the idea that she had murdered Melanie.

He should have simply left well enough alone. Brett Lassiter remained in jail, charged with murder and kidnapping, which in his opinion Lassiter deserved. Then Ronnie's words came back to haunt him. *"What if it turns out she and Lassiter worked together on the murder?" Or there was the other possibility. She had killed her mother.*

He couldn't do anything about the situation now. All he could do is wait until the session finished to learn the results.

Thirty minutes passed and the office door remained closed. He checked his watch again. Only ten minutes had gone by since he'd last checked the time. After another forty-five minutes of sitting, he needed to get some air. He left the office and walked outside to a small courtyard adjacent to the building. He keyed in Rachel's cell phone number and waited for her answer.

"What happened with the hypnosis session?" she asked.

"Nothing yet."

"Weren't you in the room?"

"I guess you could say I got blindsided. Tracy contacted Megan yesterday and asked for her representation. Tracy only wanted Megan to accompany her."

"My goodness. She must really believe she's guilty."

"I'm afraid so."

"You sound really down. I know you never believed in her guilt. There's still a chance hypnotism will prove you correct."

"Guess you're right," he said. "They ought to be finishing up pretty soon, so I'd better get back up there if I want to know the results."

"Okay, I'll see you at home later. Love you."

"Love you too."

Danny returned to the waiting room as Megan and Tracy were leaving the doctor's office. *Both smiling. Well, at least Megan looks happy. I sure hope they have good news.*

"Perfect timing," Megan said. "Everything went well."

"Exactly like you said it would," Tracy admitted. "At least I won't be going to jail." She walked closer to him and stood on tiptoes to give him a hug. "I'm sorry I doubted you."

He put his arm around her shoulder. "You sounded so certain you were guilty I began to doubt myself."

"We videoed the session and watched the tape after I came out of the trance." Tracy's voice trembled. "Which is why we were in there so long."

Megan reached in her briefcase and removed a thumb drive. "If you want to review the video, this copy is for you." She handed him the small black drive. "All we ask is that the data isn't leaked. We don't want this to appear on social media before Brett Lassiter's trial."

"Yes, please. I don't want to relive that experience in any way, shape, or form. It's bad enough my father's attorney may have to view this scene."

"Don't worry," he said. "Ronnie and I will make sure it doesn't get away from us."

Tracy's eyes widened. "Does he have to view all the gory details, too?" She wrapped her arms across her breasts.

Danny could see fear and perhaps embarrassment or shame flicker in Tracy's eyes.

"He is the sheriff," he said, softening his voice to reassure her. "If this indicates you did not kill your mother and had no connection to her death, you have nothing to fear. I understand how demeaning this might seem to you, but Ronnie will be discreet. I have control of this file. No one else will see this or hear the details from either him or me unless we're forced to disclose it to the defense attorney."

Tracy gave a tired sigh. "Thank you, Danny. Megan, I'm going to head back to my townhouse. This ordeal has left me exhausted." She started walking toward the door, then stopped. "Oh, I remembered more details about the incident in the cemetery." She looked at Megan as if for permission. "Is that okay?"

"Certainly," Megan said. "If your statement will help with the identity of those who took you and shot Susan."

Danny's heartbeat quickened. "You could have exactly what I need to charge those scumbags."

"Why don't we all go over to my office," Megan suggested. "...Or if you would be more comfortable at your place, Tracy?"

"I would. I'll see you both in about twenty minutes, if that's okay."

"Fine with me," Danny said.

"Okay with me also," Megan agreed. As soon as Tracy left the room, Megan moved closer to him and said in a low voice, "There's something else you need to know."

"What's that?"

"Brett Lassiter remained on the scene during the entire incident, but he didn't pull the trigger."

Danny clenched his fist at his side. "I should have known from that tape Wilson brought me. I figured his man would do the job by himself, so Lassiter would have the perfect alibi. Who did the shooting?"

"According to Tracy while under hypnosis, her father stood by and allowed Jeff Boudreau to beat Melanie while he tried to get her to reveal the location of the ruby. Then when she wouldn't cooperate, Lassiter ordered Boudreau to shoot her."

"Where was Tracy all this time?"

"Hiding behind a big chair. The men didn't discover her, so after the shooting they left the premises."

"And since Tracy couldn't remember many details about the murder, Lassiter started his campaign to make her believe she had killed her mother." Danny shook his head in disgust. "This presents a problem. Lassiter can always deny his presence and accuse Tracy of lying, or lay the blame fully on Boudreau."

"As a defense attorney, I can tell you this. His attorney will have a field day since the hypnosis can't be used in court and he didn't know about the planned session beforehand." Megan's expression brightened. "If he were my client, I'd want to view the video in case Tracy confessed to the crime. Your best move would be revealing the hypnosis up-front and not keeping it a secret. Tracy will not be happy, but revealing all the evidence before trial will look a lot better. If not, the prosecution being accused of concealing *any* evidence could end up blowing the case. You and Ronnie ought to make the appointment with the DA. Lassiter isn't my client, so y'all need to coordinate with him on this whole deal. I'll go along to any meeting on the subject as Tracy's representative."

"You're right. We've got the other tape recording, which is allowed in court, along with the testimony of the other defendants. It's a complicated case. I'm worried about how the jury will react. It'll be a miracle if they don't get confused."

"Yes, jury verdicts are hard to predict. I do believe with all the evidence and testimony together, DA Blanchard is more than capable of pulling off a miracle."

Forty-seven

The doctor decided to move me to a regular room instead of waiting until tomorrow. Fine with me. Josh walked alongside the stretcher as the nurse rolled me down the hospital corridor. The cart's wheels made a soft creaking sound, breaking the silence of the hallway.

The new room had a view of a courtyard bounded on three sides by two stories of hospital rooms. Much better than the confines of the ICU.

Steven arrived with a vase of flowers. He placed the bouquet on a bedside table and leaned over to give me a kiss. He extended his hand to Josh and shook hands with him.

"Megan sends her love," Steven said. "She'll visit you as soon as she can."

"Where is she?" I asked.

He gave a slight shrug. "I'm not really sure what's going on, but she's meeting with Danny and Tracy. I am certain the meeting has to do with her kidnapping and your shooting."

My interest was piqued. "I wonder if she remembered more about that day."

"What about you?" Josh asked. "Has anything come back to you about either man?"

I squeezed my eyes shut. I hated to even think about it.

"I'm sorry." Josh moved closer to the bed and clasped my hand. "I didn't mean to upset you."

"I've tried not to think about getting shot. But I have to make an attempt to recall more about those men, so they can be caught and punished."

"Yeah," Steven said, his voice angry. "I'd like to catch those SOBs."

"You and me too." Josh's angry tone and clenched fist echoed Steven's words.

"If I remember anything important, you have to promise me you will leave their capture to Danny and Ronnie." I forced a smile in an attempt to lighten the air. Both men stared at me.

"That sounds like something my grandma used to say." Josh appeared to be suppressing a smile. "You know...you asking us to let the police handle the situation because we might get hurt, when you can't resist getting involved. That's sort of like the pot calling the kettle black, isn't it?" Although his words were scolding, his tone sounded light and teasing.

Not so for my brother. Steven's laugh sounded forced and he shot me an irritated look. "That *is* it. When did you ever not get involved?" He frowned and his shoulders slumped. "Of course, if you hadn't investigated my wife's murder on your own, I'd be sitting in a prison cell at Angola. So, just for you, I'll try to control my impulse to smash their faces in if I ever meet up with them."

Josh narrowed his eyes. "Believe me, Steven, I know how you feel about smashing their faces in."

My effort to relieve the tension in the room had failed, so I directed the conversation to the unusual floral display Steven had brought.

"Roses and honeysuckle?" I pointed to the flower arrangement. "I've never seen that combination before. Where did you get them?"

"A little florist shop in the Quarter that specializes in astrological arrangements," he said. "I remembered how you used to visit your friend the clairvoyant in New Orleans, so I kinda figured you might appreciate a little New Age artistry." He indicated the symbol for a Zodiac sign embossed on a plastic stake inserted in the vase.

"Oh, are those the flowers for Gemini?" Our birthday is June 3, which falls under that sign.

"All I know is what the woman at the florist told me," he said, eyeing Josh as if for verification.

He grinned. "You couldn't prove it by me."

"I hadn't thought about Taylor Evans, my psychic friend, in quite a while," I mused. *Maybe I should consider contacting her. She may be able to give me some clues.*

Steven made an exaggerated slap to his forehead. "Oh hell. What have I done? I know that look."

"What?" I tried to look innocent.

"You're thinking about going to see her on the odd chance she can give you clues to help you remember more about your shooting so you can go find those guys. Am I right?"

"Okay, I give up. That's exactly what I was thinking."

Josh moved his gaze from me to Steven. "Speaking of psychics, how did you know what she was thinking?"

Steven and I both laughed.

"Reading each other's thoughts happens a lot with twins," I explained.

Josh chuckled. "If you say so."

Contacting Taylor might be a great idea, but I had just advised Josh and Steven to let the police handle my shooting because of the danger, yet so many times I'd gone off on my own and ended up in a serious situation. I really was the pot calling the kettle black. At least the angry atmosphere in the room had lifted.

Forty-eight

Saturday, July 26

My first visitors in the morning were Rachel and Remi. I had used Josh's cell phone last night to call Rachel with a couple of requests: my own cell phone and Harriet Haydel's journal. I had to have something to do with my time instead of watching television all day, in between the nurses coming in every so often to take my blood or my vitals.

"Hey, girl," Remi greeted me. "How are you feeling?" Her upbeat tone suggested she had recovered from her attack.

"I am improving," I admitted. "But I'll be even better when I can go home."

Rachel gave me a look of disapproval. "Hopefully, you aren't about to try to escape this time."

"Escape? You make this sound like she's in prison," Remi said.

"To her it is." Rachel moved her head in my direction.

I gave an exaggerated sigh. "All right ladies. I'm not that bad, am I?"

Their lack of comment answered my question.

"I'm serious," Rachel said. "You can't leave here until the doctor discharges you. I know what happened the first time with Doctor

Theriot, but I can't imagine how you talked Doctor Richard into letting you leave his office without at least doing lab work."

"Isn't he about ready to retire?" Remi asked.

"He's old, but I don't believe he's senile," Rachel said.

"He was rushed that day. His office was packed." I leaned back against the pillows. Rachel was really on the warpath against me. "I promise I will not try to leave here until Doctor Theriot releases me. That's one lesson I've learned from all of this."

"Good." Rachel reached into her big purse and retrieved my cell phone and Harriet's journal. "We ran into Steven and Josh on our way in. Were they here all night?"

"Yes, they were. I sent them home." I got a curious look from Rachel. "They'd been here all night. They needed to rest and get something to eat."

"Gramps said he would come by later with good news," Remi said. "He didn't say what the good news was about, but I believe he's identified the man who shot you."

My heart beat faster. "I hope you're correct. Have you heard anything about the person who attacked you?"

She shook her head. "All I know is the man is suspected to be one of the Wilsons."

"I thought the man who shot me was also one of them. As it turns out, he happens to be part of Brett Lassiter's group." I frowned. "We don't know which one yet. Maybe that's Danny's news."

Remi's cell phone vibrated. She checked the display. "Oh, I need to take this." She stepped out of the room and into the hallway.

Rachel moved closer to my bed. "Sorry if I came on too strong back there. I've been worried about you. This case has been like no other. First, Danny got shot. Then someone shot you and kidnapped Tracy."

"Not to mention Remi being attacked," I said.

Her eyes teared up as she took hold of my hand. "I think of you not only as a friend, but as a daughter. I don't want anything to happen to you."

"I should apologize for worrying you. You have been my dearest friend ever since Jim and I moved to Cypress Lake." I felt myself tearing up. "I promise I'll do better. But I'm going to be fine. So let's change the subject before this breaks down into a tear fest."

She smiled. "Agreed."

The door to my room opened slowly. I expected to see Remi returning after her phone call. My parents walked cautiously inside as if they were about to witness an awful scene. What in the world did they expect to see?

Forty-nine

Rachel stood and greeted my parents with a smile. "It's good to see you."

My father returned her smile and shook her hand. Mother remained silent, but gave a half smile. Something didn't seem right with her. Could she be sick? Or was I responsible for causing her to have a nervous breakdown? I suppose I'm a parent's worst nightmare. And I'm actually an adult.

Rachel excused herself. "I'll let y'all visit with Susan." To me she added, "I need to check on Remi, since she hasn't returned from taking that phone call."

"Okay." I felt a bit awkward, expecting a barrage of criticism from Mother at least, and maybe even Dad, who hardly ever raised his voice.

My father, ever the peacemaker, drew closer and leaned over to kiss me. "You look better than expected. You even have a little color in your cheeks."

I smiled. "Thanks, Dad. I am feeling a lot better. This time I intend to follow the doctor's orders and not try to leave the hospital before he thinks I'm ready." I turned my gaze to Mother. "I hope you're not so angry with me that I don't rate a kiss?"

She gave a sigh of what seemed like relief. "No, of course not. I'm happy you're feeling better. You gave us quite the scare." She gave me a kiss on the cheek and squeezed my hand.

"I scared myself. I should have stayed in the hospital the first time instead of talking Doctor Theriot into releasing me before he thought I was ready."

Surprisingly, Mother didn't respond with one of her usual retorts.

"I'm glad you're following his orders now," she said. "Your father and I don't want to lose you or your brother."

Guess I'm always looking for a mystery in everything, but her words sounded strange to me. "Was I in such serious condition you were afraid I might not make it?"

Dad answered my question. "Yes, when you needed more surgery and had to be given blood, we knew your condition was serious. You were lucky Steven shares your blood type."

I brushed off my strange vibes. "Yeah, I'm lucky he was there for me."

We visited for a while and I shared photos on my phone of the twins. Normal family stuff. My relationship with my parents, especially my mother, hadn't been normal for years.

I mulled over their visit for a long time after they left. Shaking off my questions about statements both of them had made, I picked up Harriet's journal and began to read.

The first two pages didn't produce any earthshaking clues. The next entry in the book caught my eye. It turned out to be the one leading up to an answer as to whether she had pushed Charles off the balcony.

July 4, 1930

For months and months Charles has been perpetually drunk. Nothing I could say to him would prevent the bourbon from flowing into his glass. And holidays like today were the worst, with many houseguests also imbibing. This, of course, is not to my liking, especially as it is against the law. I hesitate to say this, but the crash of the stock market and our financial losses were more than enough to drive anyone to drink. There have been times when even I have been tempted to lose myself in alcohol. My parents would have been in a state of shock if I had done so. Neither prohibition nor the hard times the nation is going through can stop the illegal sale or the consumption of liquor. At least not in this area. I have to assume the rest of the country and perhaps the world is also experiencing an economic downturn and the unlawful production of alcohol. Although I've heard liquor was being smuggled in from Canada, so drink may not be illegal there.

July 5, 1930

    I discovered Charles' body by accident early this morning when I went out on the balcony to have my tea. The servants said they heard me scream, although I don't recall doing so. He lay on the ground below the balcony. Most likely he lost his balance in his drunken state and fell to his death. I didn't want to think he had killed himself, but death by suicide was more than possible, considering his depression.

    In his hand I discovered the velvet drawstring bag in which he kept the ruby. I secreted the bag away before the authorities arrived or anyone else found it and was tempted to steal the cursed gem. What I would do with the ruby I hadn't decided yet. I'd like to throw the stone in the river. There has been nothing but trouble since Charles bought it from the man in Rangoon. For now, I must begin to prepare for his funeral.

What had she done with the ruby? Her journal ended after this last entry, so I'd never know what became of the supposedly cursed ruby.

Fifty

Danny strode into my hospital room with Josh and Megan following him. All three looked pleased at whatever news they'd learned before coming up to the hospital. Well, I couldn't really speak for Megan. I didn't know her part in this little conference, but I suspected Tracy was involved.

Josh had called me before his arrival to let me know he had been updated on the latest investigation. He wouldn't tell me the details because Danny wanted to tell me himself.

I sat up straight in the bed. "Okay, fill me in. Everyone looks pleased with the results. Give me some good news."

The trio crowded around me. Being the center of attention, I felt a bit awkward, but I was so ready to hear good news. "Let's have it."

Danny spoke first. "The man who shot you was Jeff Boudreau."

"The man you interviewed a few days ago?" I asked. "As I recall, his DNA was on cigarette butts at the cemetery."

"Right. Believe it or not, he eventually confessed. He said he didn't mean to shoot you. The gun accidentally went off." Danny made a face indicating his disbelief in the man's statement.

"The nerve of this guy. Are you serious?" I almost choked on my anger.

"Take it easy," he said. "That's just standard procedure for a shooter who wants to minimize his part in the crime."

"I assume he worked for Brett Lassiter."

"That's a given. Lassiter had already admitted he'd arranged to have Tracy kidnapped. But for her own good. To protect her, since she killed her mother. He claimed he'd warned Boudreau not to do any shooting."

I rolled my eyes. "Yeah, right."

"That's what I said," Josh chimed in. "Lassiter was the mastermind behind the whole deal."

Megan agreed. "They all want to keep from being labeled as monsters." She glanced at Danny before turning to me. "There's news concerning Tracy."

"Is she all right?"

"She will be eventually," Megan said. "Danny had arranged a hypnosis session for her to see if she could remember the events of the night her mother was murdered."

My chest tightened. "She didn't kill her, I hope."

"Definitely not. She witnessed her mother being beaten and then shot. The effect of alcohol and marijuana in her system and witnessing such a traumatic event caused her to block out portions of that night in her memory."

"Has her father confessed to the murder?" I expected a negative on that point.

"Yes, he finally confessed to arranging the murder and being on the premises, but said he didn't shoot her," Danny said.

My heart raced. "You said it wasn't Tracy. Then who?"

Danny's jaw muscle tightened. "Jeff Boudreau. I knew Lassiter wouldn't have done the job himself."

I shook my head in disbelief.

"A positive outcome was uncertain for a while, after Lassiter's attorney was informed about the hypnosis session and that there was video." He waved a hand in Megan's direction. "You want to tell the rest of the story?"

She shrugged. "All I did was go along with you and Ronnie to the meeting with the DA. He contacted Mr. Lassiter's attorney to join us. After viewing the video, he agreed to consult Mr. Lassiter about pleading guilty, so there would be no trial." She smiled. "I'm thrilled he did. Unfortunately, Tracy will need therapy to recover from all of this."

I'm pretty sure I will also need therapy after this.

"Did he get a plea deal? I hope not," I said.

"Only to take the death penalty off the table," Megan said.

I turned my attention to Danny. "What about all the Wilsons?"

"All the family members who played any part in this whole affair have been charged, including Russell Wilson. He's the one who shot at Tracy and me in front of the court house and tried to attack Remi. Joey Chin was the young man you encountered in the cemetery." He glanced at Josh, and then continued, "The one piece of this puzzle we couldn't find was who caused the death of Josh's cousin, Jack Broussard. His death was for sure connected to the Anne LeBlanc hit-and-run case. As I told Josh earlier, the Jennings PD and the parish sheriff said he's welcome to come look at their files on the incident if he wants to do some investigating on his own. They don't have the funds or manpower to pursue a cold case at present."

"I talked to both men right before I came up here," Josh acknowledged. "I told them it would be a few months before I could get up there, but I definitely wanted to look into his death."

I reached for Harriet's journal. "I discovered more about Charles Haydel's death. Although Harriet's entry doesn't prove he wasn't murdered, she is eliminated as a suspect in my mind." I read the two entries aloud to them.

"I'll bet she buried the ruby with him," Josh said.

"Me, too," I said. "That's kind of what I was thinking."

"Maybe so," Danny agreed. "But be careful. If that idea ever went public, there would be people trying to dig up his grave."

"Unfortunately, you're right," I said. "Human beings go wild at the thought of finding treasure."

"True." Danny grinned. "So, to paraphrase an old saying, we should let sleeping rubies lie."

Groans sounded from the rest of us.

Fifty-one

Sunday, July 27

I was finishing my breakfast when Rachel arrived. Sitting in a chair was a nice change from trying to get positioned right in my bed in order to manage food and drink.

"Oh my, they have you out of bed," she said. "You must be improving. How's the food?"

I shrugged. "Not bad for hospital food. This time I think the doctor is trying to get me out of here instead of the other way around. He moved me to this room earlier than he'd first told me."

She pointed a finger at me. "No, this is how you should have proceeded in the first hospital stay. Gradually working up to being strong enough to go home. He'll probably keep you only a few more days."

"You're right," I admitted. "I'm still not back to normal yet, but I'm getting there." I reached over to the bed and grabbed Harriet's journal. "Did Danny tell you about the last two entries in here?"

"He mentioned something about the possibility that she'd buried the ruby with her husband after he died. He said he'd leave it up to you to give me the details."

I turned to the correct page and handed the book to her. "Here, read these."

She read the entries and sat in silence for a long moment. "This more or less rules out the possibility she pushed him to his death."

"It still doesn't rule out the possibility someone else did. But I suppose we won't solve the mystery of his death or what happened to the ruby unless more evidence shows up."

"Some mysteries are unsolvable," Rachel said. "On the other hand, all the other deaths in this family were solved."

"There's another mystery of sorts to which I'd like to find answers. I want to know all about the Wilsons' family connections on down the line."

"I suspect that some of them might be the result of extramarital affairs by men in the family," she said. "It would be interesting to discover information about the other affairs and any connections they might have to the Wilsons or any other family. For example, Carl LeBlanc and his mistress. And then there's the boy Charles Haydel had with one of the Burmese nannies. That may be a lifetime project."

"The illegitimate kids idea was something along the same line as what I'm thinking. Danny mentioned some of their names yesterday." I shook my head. "You're right. Looking into their history would take forever. I'll think about the Wilsons and the others if I ever don't have anything else to do." I hoped to get a laugh out of Rachel, but instead she narrowed her eyes.

"Russell Wilson shot Danny and he's also the one who attacked Remi. I'm glad he was arrested and charged." An uncertain look crossed her face. "I can only pray he gets convicted."

I widened my eyes. "Are you worried he won't?"

She looked away for a second. "You never can tell these days. There's always the chance for one person to vote not guilty because he or she feels sorry for him. You know...he had such a hard life."

Caught off guard by the intensity of her words, all I could think to say was, "I've never heard you express those concerns."

Her shoulders slumped. "Sorry, I didn't mean to bring such negativity into our conversation." She changed the subject. "How was the visit with your parents?"

"Okay, I guess." I tried being nonchalant. "Mother didn't chew me out for having to return to the hospital."

"What about your father? How did he react?"

I smiled. "He told me I looked better than expected. He said I even had some color in my cheeks."

She gave a soft laugh. "He was right about your appearance. When I visited you yesterday, your color looked a lot better than the day before."

"I'm feeling better."

"What did your mother have to say about everything that's happened?" Rachel asked. "You said she didn't chew you out."

"When my parents first discovered I had been shot, Dad phoned me. He scolded me a little about getting into such serious trouble. Nothing unusual about his reaction, but he insisted I speak to my mother." I told Rachel about our conversation and how I had gotten into a shouting match with her. "This time she kissed me and squeezed my hand. She also said I'd given them a scare."

"Maybe she didn't give you her usual spiel because they believe they almost lost you."

"That's possible, but both made statements that on the surface seemed normal. Perhaps I see mystery in everything that's not the usual." I shook my head. "I don't know. I'll just leave well enough alone unless something surprising or unusual happens in connection with my parents."

Although I'd said I would accept my parents' words at face value, I found doing so difficult. All the talk about how fortunate I was that Steven was able to give me blood seemed far out. Why wouldn't he be able to donate blood for me? Or donate an organ? We're twins. Not identical twins, but still, Dad's statement bothered me. Even if our blood types didn't match, I could always receive type O.

On Sunday evening, I got antsy. The nurse allowed me to walk down the hallway dragging my IV machine beside me. My legs still felt shaky, but I figured the more I used them other than for making a trip to the bathroom now and then, my strength would be back in no time. But I couldn't very well go on any long walks in the park today.

I decided to question Doctor Theriot when he came by in the morning about when he planned on releasing me. Glancing at the IV, I thought of how great it would be not to drag that contraption around with me every time I got out of bed.

The door opened to my room. I expected a family member or friend, but Doctor Theriot surprised me. His ears must have been burning. I certainly didn't expect to see him until tomorrow.

"I wanted to let you know about a few tests I've ordered for you tomorrow," he said.

"Does that mean I'm not going home tomorrow?" My disappointment must have shown.

He waved his hand as if dismissing my concern. "Not necessarily. I ordered blood work and a scan on your shoulder to make sure you're healing properly. Now," he added, "I don't want you to get too excited yet, but if the tests are good, I'll discharge you later in the day tomorrow."

I couldn't help but smile. "Not that I don't like y'all up here, but I am past ready to leave."

"I get that a lot from my patients," he said with a poker face. "You know it goes both ways. After I discharge you, I don't want to see you up here again any time soon. Get some rest and we'll talk tomorrow."

I hoped not to be back in the hospital ever again. Given my history, I guess that was unrealistic.

Fifty-two

Monday, July 28

At two in the afternoon, the doctor officially released me from the hospital. No one could imagine how relieved I was to be going home.

Completely dressed, I sat on the side of the bed waiting for Josh's arrival. Male voices outside the partially open door caught my attention. They sounded familiar, but I couldn't quite place them.

Two totally unexpected visitors strode into the room: Jim's old NOPD buddies, Phil Berthelot and Dave Falcon, Phil dressed casually in khaki pants, a blue polo shirt and athletic footwear and Dave wearing expensive-looking gray slacks along with a pink dress shirt and gray Italian loafers. Together they made quite the odd pair.

"Looks like we got here just in time to see you," Phil said. "Are you being discharged?"

"Yes, thank goodness. What a surprise to see you guys." *I'll bet Josh will be surprised as well.*

"With all the shootings around here, we thought we needed to check up on everybody," Falcon said. "I understand Danny took a bullet in the arm and then you. What's going on?"

"It's a long story, but all the bad guys have been charged and put in jail where they belong."

"I thought we owed it to Jim to check on you," Falcon said.

I frowned. "As you can see, I'm doing quite well."

He apparently picked up on my sarcasm. He glanced down at the floor for a short moment.

"I heard you met Josh Broussard at the seminar in Baton Rouge," I said.

Falcon nodded. "Yes, I did. He's a nice guy."

I eyed him with a steady gaze. "I'm glad you approve. He is a great guy."

Phil shifted his weight from one foot to the other, then cleared his throat. "We're not going to stay. Just wanted to make sure you were okay." He jerked his head toward Falcon. "Time for us to leave."

"Yeah, guess you're right," Falcon replied and walked out of the room.

Phil moved closer to me and said in a low voice, "I was concerned about you. Getting shot is nothing to fool around with. I'm relieved you're doing well." His expression sobered. "If we upset you, I apologize. I personally am glad you're moving on with your life."

"Why did Dave think he owed it to Jim to check up on me?"

He shook his head. "I have no idea what's going on in his damn mind. I think he's having a midlife crisis. He's been single too long."

"It's good to see you, Phil. Give my regards to your wife."

"Thanks. Gracie will be happy to hear you're on the mend."

I watched him as he walked out the door. Phil was such a sweetheart. I'd always had a fondness for him. His last statement made me wonder if Dave had entertained thoughts of dating me. I didn't like the idea.

Dave had always impressed me as being conceited and maybe even a little odd. He'd always dressed in expensive suits and driven a fancy sports car. Not your typical detective.

Josh walked into the room with a strange look on his face. "I ran into…"

"Dave Falcon and Phil Berthelot," I finished. "They just left."

"They came to check on you, I presume."

"Yes, they only stayed a few minutes. Were you introduced to Phil?"

"Yeah, he seems like a real down-to-earth guy. I can't say as much for his partner." He gave me a cautious glance.

"Neither can I. Now let's drop the subject of Dave Falcon and get me out of here."

A faint smile moved his lips. "Fine by me."

Fifty-three

Thursday, August 5

Almost two weeks ago, I was released from the hospital. During that time, I always felt shaky in the morning, but after an hour or so, all that disappeared. I really must be on the mend. Physically, that is. Emotionally I'm not so sure.

This morning the twins left for their first day of school. Hard to believe they're starting the fourth grade this year. The August start of school in the state began a number of years ago to make up for any lost time due to hurricanes or other weather phenomenon. No one likes the idea of such an early start, except maybe parents who need quiet time after two straight months of dealing with their kids.

Since the kids were in school, I decided to go shopping. I needed to add cooler weather clothes to my wardrobe, although the weather in Louisiana doesn't get cooler until at least October. We just have to be prepared for small cold fronts that dry up the humidity and give us a low temperature of fifty degrees for about three mornings. After that, we're back to hot and humid until the next front arrives.

As I started for the door, my cell phone rang. The call was from my father. I assumed he was only calling to check on my recovery progress. I thought about ignoring the call until I returned, but my inner voice told me I needed to answer.

"Hi Dad," I said. "I was just about to leave the house to go shopping."

"If you're going shopping you must be cured."

I gave a soft laugh. "I'm getting better all the time. So, what's up with you?"

He paused for a long moment. "Your mother and I want you and Steven to come over to the house tonight. There's something we need to discuss with you and your brother."

I frowned. "This sounds serious. Are y'all okay?"

"We're fine, health-wise. The business we need to discuss is a subject we don't want to talk about over the phone. I've already spoken to Steven. Come over about seven-thirty, if that's okay."

"I assume the twins aren't invited to this meeting," I said.

"We would prefer not. After we have our discussion, you and Steven are free to tell anyone you choose. We'll see you this evening." He ended the call before I had a chance to object or comment.

My phone rang again immediately. "Yes, I got the call from Dad. Do you know what this meeting concerns?"

"Hell if I know," Steven answered. "I guess we'll find out. I'll come pick you up about six-fifteen or so."

"Fine, see you then." I held the phone in my hand for a while, mulling over this out-of-the-blue meeting our parents had called.

~ * ~

Anxiety hung in the air inside Steven's car on the way to our parents' house. I couldn't concentrate on any line of conversation. My thoughts flipped from one scene to another like there was a slide show in my head. I couldn't imagine what the subject of the meeting could be. In our previous conversations, Dad kept denying any illness or trouble between him and Mother.

Upon arriving at the house, I didn't get out of the car at first. Finally, Steven came around to the passenger side and opened the door.

"Come on," he urged. "This can't be all that bad."

"I have the feeling they aren't going to tell us they won the lottery." I reluctantly followed him inside the house.

My mother appeared nervous when she ushered Steven and me toward the living room, a room only used on special occasions or to have serious or private conversations. I received another surprise upon entering. Aunt Rose, our mother's sister, stood from her seat on the sofa and greeted us each with a hug.

Confused, I glanced back at my parents. "Is something wrong?"

Steven echoed my question.

"Please have a seat." Dad's usually calm voice sounded strained. "We'll explain everything."

Once everyone was seated, Mother was the first to speak. "You're confused and perhaps fearful about what's going on. I can assure you of a few things. Neither Charles nor I are sick with an incurable disease. We're not getting a divorce, nor are we in any kind of trouble, financial or otherwise."

I thought it odd that she addressed Dad as Charles. She always referred to him as "Father" or "your father" when speaking to me or Steven.

Mother exchanged a glance with her sister and then directed her gaze to me. "I know I've given you a great deal of grief about your activities ever since you were a child. In my mind, the admonitions were for your own good." She paused for a short moment, then took a deep breath. "Susan, you are the image of our younger sister, along with your personality. I also see a lot of her personality characteristics in you, Steven, but not as strongly as with Susan." Her voice cracked and tears glistened in her eyes.

My heart thumped. "What does your sister have to do with why we're here? Actually, I never even knew you had a younger sister."

Dad gave me a look that said, "Shut up and let your mother talk." Although he would have said the words in a more polite way. Steven put his hand on my arm, his silent signal to me to let her finish.

Mother's face paled. She shook her head. Aunt Rose sat up straight on the edge of her seat.

"I'll finish the story." She turned her gaze to my mother, who gave her assent.

I couldn't imagine where all this was leading. I'd never seen Mother upset like this before.

"Yes," Aunt Rose said. "We had a sister much younger than Elizabeth and me. Her name was Catherine. She left home at sixteen and headed off for parts unknown. We all suspected New Orleans and the French Quarter. However, no matter how long and hard we searched, she couldn't be located."

She brushed a lock of salt and pepper hair away from her forehead, a reminder of a habit of my cousin Melanie, her daughter, who had the same errant lock of hair.

"One day in June of nineteen seventy-six, our daddy received a phone call from the New Orleans police about a pregnant girl who had been shot. A police officer had found her, barely alive. She told him her name and who to notify. By the time she arrived at the hospital, she was in a coma. She never recovered."

"What happened to her baby?" Steven asked.

"Babies...a set of twins was delivered that night by C-section."

I took in a deep breath. I suddenly knew where all this was headed. "Steven and me?"

Aunt Rose's lower lip trembled. "No one wanted you to go into foster care, but John and I were expecting..." Her voice trailed off.

I couldn't speak for seconds, minutes...I don't know how long I sat in stunned silence. Steven looked equally dumbfounded.

Finally, Mother spoke. "I couldn't have children, but our sister's babies were orphaned, so Charles and I adopted you two."

Steven beat me to asking an important question before my shocked vocal cords could respond.

"Why are you only telling us this now?" His voice had a sharp edge.

I couldn't blame him for being angry. The news was a lot to take in.

"We decided to tell you the truth after Susan's surgery," Dad continued. "The possibility of blood transfusions or organ replacements might be needed in the future. Not just for you two, but perhaps Matthew and Caroline also. We're not well versed in these medical issues. I don't know…these issues may not pose any problems in the future. However, we decided the secret had been kept way too long. You deserved to know the truth."

Questions swirled around in my head. Who was our biological father? Was he the person who killed our birth mother?

Dad's expression clouded as he answered my unspoken questions to a certain degree. "As to your true father, he remains unidentified. We don't know if he killed Catherine or if someone else murdered her."

He must have read my mind. Finding out the two people Steven and I had known all our lives as our mother and father were not our biological parents hit hard. I could tell my brother felt the same.

I leaned back in the chair and closed my eyes. Something Dad had said resonated in my mind. He was our true father and always would be. We have Mother's family blood running through our bodies. The identification of our biological father may never be known and our mother had died from gun violence.

My gunshot wound had most likely prompted this big reveal. If Mother had feared all my life I would end up like her sister, my real mother, I understood why they'd decided to tell us the truth. Now I also understood why there existed what I'd thought of as a rift between Mother and me.

I looked at them and felt only love. Tears filled my eyes. I wiped them away with my hand and made eye contact with Steven. He appeared to have the same idea. "Mother, you and Dad are our real parents."

Steven acknowledged my statement. We both met them in the center of the room. Lots of *I love yous* and hugs came easily. Aunt Rose got in on the hugs, too. A meeting that had started out ominously with family secrets being revealed ended with a lot of family love.

On the drive back to Cypress Lake, Steven and I rode in silence most of the way. I had a lot to think about. I imagine Steven did also.

The irony of the story hit me almost as hard as the gunshot had. The event when Steven and I made our entrance into the world had involved a murder mystery. A mystery too close to home to ignore.

He glanced at me. "Aren't you curious about the identity of our biological father? Our birth mother was murdered. I figure that's right up your alley. Are you going to look into the story?"

"Of course, I'm curious. Most likely sometime in the near future I'll start trying to track down him and our mother's killer. For now, his identity is a mystery to solve another day," I said. "There's a project I need to do before I start another investigation. I've been considering speaking to a therapist about all my feelings and actions. I need counseling."

"You can do both at the same time."

"Am I to assume you want me to start right away on finding out our birth parents' story?"

"Why not? I want to know, too."

"I need to get my head on straight before I start a search." His cajoling had started to work on me. The suspense of an unsolved mystery bubbled up inside me.

He appeared skeptical about my hesitation to dive into a murder mystery so close to our family. "I don't believe for one minute you're going to let this wait until months down the road," he said. "I'll bet you get on your computer as soon as you walk in the door at your house."

I punched him in the arm. "You know me too well."

Meet A. C. Mason

A C Mason is a Louisiana native and resident. She's a mother, grandmother, and great-grandmother of three. Her two daughters and their families live in nearby communities. She grew up reading Nancy Drew, Trixie Beldon, and other mysteries for girls. Her love of a good mystery led her to write her own. She's a member of Sisters-in-Crime.

A very spoiled cat named Wiley shares her home. A former cat named Katy (2000-2017) makes appearances in all her Susan Foret mystery series as the protagonist's pet.

Works From The Pen Of A. C. Mason

<u>April Fools</u> - Susan Foret, an aspiring mystery writer, takes on a real life mystery when she tries to prove her brother didn't murder his wife.

<u>Mardi Gras Gris Gris</u> - Susan Foret is again thrust into a murder scene when one of the town's wealthiest citizens dies near her as the local Krewe's parade is ending.

<u>Deadly Bayou</u> - Police chief Jim Foret's death is ruled a suicide. Susan Foret believes her husband has been murdered and sets out to prove his death is a homicide.

<u>The Mistletoe Murders</u> - Oak Point, Louisiana homicide detective Caleb Bourque is tasked with solving the case of a serial killer who leaves an unusual calling card with each victim—a sprig of mistletoe. After Joanna Chatelaine, a co-founder of a women's outreach center, is killed, her sister Jamie starts receiving threats to her life if she doesn't close Magdalen House.
Can Caleb unravel this complicated case before the killer makes good on his threat to kill Jamie?

<u>A Grievous Sin</u> - The discovery of a body leads Susan Foret into the world of illegal immigrants and smuggled artifacts and jewels, including an antique emerald cross from a sunken Spanish galleon.

Letter to Our Readers

Enjoy this book?

You can make a difference.

As an independent publisher, Wings ePress, Inc. does not have the financial clout of the large New York publishers. We can't afford large magazine spreads or subway posters to tell people about our quality books.

But we do have something much more effective and powerful than ads. We have a large base of loyal readers.

Honest reviews help bring the attention of new readers to our books.

If you enjoyed this book, we would appreciate it if you would spend a few minutes posting a review on the site where you purchased this book or on the Wings ePress, Inc. webpages at:

https://wingsepress.com/

Thank You

Visit Our Website

For The Full Inventory
Of Quality Books:

Wings ePress.Inc
https://wingsepress.com/

Quality trade paperbacks and downloads
in multiple formats,
in genres ranging from light romantic comedy
to general fiction and horror.
Wings has something for every reader's taste.
Visit the website, then bookmark it.
We add new titles each month!

Wings ePress Inc.
3000 N. Rock Road
Newton, KS 67114